Dear Reader,

Beginning with the that I will be bringing you my real name of Joan Elliott Pickart. I hope you've enjoyed the books I've written for Silhouette as Robin Elliott, but it's time for Robin to step aside and allow *me* to come into your homes.

I've received many letters over the years asking me how I came to choose the name Robin Elliott. I have three daughters: Tracey, Robin and Paige. As a mother, I could never pick one over the other, so I asked the editors at Silhouette to do it. Since the names Tracey and Paige belonged to other authors, I was told "Welcome to Silhouette, Robin Elliott!"

Many years and many books have passed since that day, and I want to thank you all for your wonderful and continued support. You, the loyal readers, are the ones who make it all possible. All of you—around the country and the world—are very special to me.

Warmest regards,

Joan Elliott Pickart

Dear Reader,

For many years you have known and loved Silhouette author Robin Elliott. But did you know she is also popular romance writer Joan Elliott Pickart? Now she has chosen to write her Silhouette books using the Joan Elliott Pickart name, which is also her real name!

You'll be reading the same delightful stories you've grown to love from "Robin Elliott," only now, keep an eye out for Joan Elliott Pickart. Joan's first book using her real name is this month's *Man of the Month*. It's called *Angels and Elves,* and it's the first in her BABY BET series. What exactly is a "baby bet"? Well, you'll have to read to find out, but I assure you—it's a lot of fun!

November also marks the return to Silhouette Books of popular writer Kristin James, with her first Silhouette Desire title, *Once in a Blue Moon*. I'm thrilled that Kristin has chosen to be part of the Desire family, and I know her many fans can't wait to read this sexy love story.

Some other favorites are also in store for you this month: Jennifer Greene, Jackie Merritt and Lass Small. And a new writer is always a treat—new writers are the voices of tomorrow, after all! This month, Pamela Ingrahm makes her writing debut...and I hope we'll see many more books from this talented new author.

Until next month, happy reading!

Lucia Macro
Senior Editor

Please address questions and book requests to:
Silhouette Reader Service
U.S.: 3010 Walden Ave., P.O. Box 1325, Buffalo, NY 14269
Canadian: P.O. Box 609, Fort Erie, Ont. L2A 5X3

JOAN ELLIOTT PICKART
ANGELS AND ELVES

SILHOUETTE *Desire*®
Published by Silhouette Books
America's Publisher of Contemporary Romance

SILHOUETTE BOOKS

ISBN 0-373-05961-2

ANGELS AND ELVES

JOAN ELLIOTT PICKART

is the author of over sixty-five novels. When she isn't writing, she enjoys watching football, knitting, reading, gardening and attending craft shows on the town square. Joan has three daughters and a fantastic little grandson. Her three dogs and one cat allow her to live with them in a cozy cottage in a charming, small town in the high pine country of Arizona.

For my then-agent, Robin Kaigh,
and for
my now-agent, Laurie Feigenbaum.
Thank you, friends.

Prologue

Forrest MacAllister stopped in the doorway to the living room and looked at the woman stretched out on the sofa with pillows propped behind her back to allow her to sit up. She was deeply engrossed in the novel she was reading, and was unaware of Forrest's presence.

Andrea, he mused. His baby sister was a beautiful woman. Her auburn curls were in fetching disarray, and her dark brown eyes were clear and sparkling. The best part, though, was the pure joy, the happiness-to-the-maximum that he could actually feel emanating from her.

She also had, he decided, the largest, roundest stomach he'd ever seen. Twins definitely took up a lot of space in a pregnant lady. Yep, his baby sister was *definitely* awaiting the arrival of her own babies. Big time.

"So what's new, kid?" he asked, breaking the serene silence in the room.

Andrea's head snapped up and a smile instantly appeared on her face.

"Forrest! Oh, my gosh, you're really home. Give me a million hugs. I didn't hear you come into the house."

"John let me in as he was leaving," Forrest said, crossing the room. "Your husband is looking like a proper and prosperous Yuppie." He leaned over and hugged her, then straightened again to meet her gaze. "This is very efficient. I can hug three people at once."

Andrea laughed. "Aren't I awful? I'm impersonating a beached whale. And now I'm confined to either bed, sofa or chair, so these little darlings don't arrive too soon."

"You look fantastic."

"Fat. The word is *fat*. Sit, sit. I want to look at you until I'm cross-eyed. Oh, Forrest, I'm so glad you're back from Japan in time to be here when the babies are born. A year is much too long for you to be away. We all missed you terribly."

"I missed you, too, but it was quite an experience, and one I'll always remember. Japan is beautiful, Andrea, it really is. And it was a tremendous challenge to design a house that would blend in, yet have all the features the client wanted."

"Your letters were super, even if you still can't spell worth a darn," she said.

Forrest chuckled. "Spelling is a hopeless endeavor for me." He yawned. "I have jet lag so bad I don't even know what day it is. I came straight here from the airport, but Mom and Dad are going to have to settle for a phone call until after I get some sleep."

"And our brothers. You'd better call them, too. Michael and Ryan are so glad you're coming home for good."

"That's enough travel for me for a while. Listen, I really do need to get some sleep. I just wanted to stop by and make sure you were doing all right. You're staying put like the doctor said, aren't you?"

"Oh, yes. I'm grumpy and bored, and my darling John has the patience of a saint. But I'm following orders so that the twins have every chance to be healthy.

"Forrest, before you go I'd like to talk to you about something. It won't take long."

"Fire away."

"Well, you know that my favorite author is Jillian Jones-Jenkins, and that I met her several years ago at Deedee Hamilton's store, Books and Books. We've all become good friends since then."

Forrest nodded. "Jillian writes those gooey romance novels you read."

"Don't start. It's extremely bad form to hassle expectant mothers. Anyway, Jillian is arriving home tomorrow from a lengthy autographing tour and is doing a signing at Deedee's store as a special favor. Forrest, please, would you go to the store, buy Jillian's new book, and have her autograph it for me?" Andrea begged.

"Why? Deedee will be right there. Can't she do it? As far as that goes, Jillian could bring you a copy. Since you're friends, and you can't go out, surely she'll come visit you."

"Well—" Andrea smiled brightly "—there's a little more to it than that."

"Uh-oh. Not good," Forrest said. "You have that look in your eyes that says you're up to something. Ever since we were kids, that gleam got *me* in trouble."

"Forrest, Forrest, this is me, Andrea, your adorable, sweet little sister. I'm simply asking you to do me a teeny-tiny favor."

"Spare me," he said, rolling his eyes heavenward. "I've fallen for your innocent routine so many times, it's a crime."

"Keep an open mind," she said. "You're not going back to work for a bit. Right?"

"Right," he said, eyeing her warily. "I'm planning to take a couple of weeks off. I usually worked seven days a week in Japan."

"Perfect. You see, Deedee and I are very worried about Jillian. She's been on this exhausting tour and she was tired even before she left. Why was she tired? I'm glad you asked."

"I didn't."

"Hush. Jillian seems to have forgotten how to relax, have fun, have a proper balance of work and play in her life. She's gotten so caught up in deadlines and her writing schedule, that we hardly see her. We can't pry her out of the office in her house."

"And?"

"Remember when the four of us were kids and Mom would periodically say it was time for her Angels and Elves to get busy?"

"Yeah, I remember. We'd mow the lawn for an elderly couple, run errands for a shut-in, you'd baby-sit for free for a new mother, stuff like that. Every few months we did Angels and Elves assignments."

"Exactly. Forrest, Deedee and I are asking you to make Jillian Jones-Jenkins your Angels and Elves assignment. Take her out, have fun, get her to relax and enjoy life again. Hopefully she'll realize how narrow her existence has become."

"Oh, man," Forrest said, frowning, "are you kidding? That's nuts, Andrea. I don't even know this woman. You expect *me* to convince her to get her priorities back in order? That's the dumbest Angels and Elves assignment I've ever heard."

"It is not. It's custom-made for you. You have some free time right now. You're handsome, charming, intelligent, all that jazz. And you know how to show a woman a good time. Heaven knows, you've got women chasing after you like bees to honey."

"Flattery will get you nothing."

"Don't say no. At least promise me you'll think about it."

"Andrea . . ."

"Please?"

"Okay, okay," he said, raising both hands. "I'll think about it."

"Good."

"For about five seconds. Then I'll say no."

"Darn it, Forrest, don't be so difficult. Look, go to Books and Books tomorrow and buy Jillian's new novel for me. You can meet her at the same time."

"*Then* I'll say no. Andrea, has it ever occurred to you that Jillian might not appreciate the sneaky little program you and Deedee are putting together here?"

"It's for her own good. Deedee and I really are concerned about her. She won't know you're on an Angels and Elves assignment. This is a very humanitarian mission I'm asking you to undertake, Forrest."

He got to his feet.

"I'll go buy the book," he said, "and meet Jillian. Beyond that? I'm not promising anything. I'm thirty-two years old. A person would think that I'd have learned by now that your schemes always spell trouble for me in big, bold letters. I shouldn't be going anywhere near Deedee Hamilton's store."

"But you will, and you're wonderful, and I adore you, and I'm so glad you're home."

"Yeah, yeah," he said, laughing, "and you've been able to wrap me around your little finger since the day you were born." He leaned over and kissed her on the forehead. "Bye for now, brat. Take good care of the dynamic duo you're toting around in there."

"Bye, Forrest. And thank you."

Andrea waited until she heard the front door click shut behind Forrest, then snatched up the receiver of the telephone that had been placed on the coffee table within her reach. She pushed buttons in rapid succession.

"Deedee? Forrest was just here. He wouldn't give me a definite yes, but I talked him out of a definite no. Here's the setup. Forrest will come to your store tomorrow to buy Jillian's new book for me and..."

One

Best wishes, Jillian Jones-Jenkins.

Jillian stared at the words she had just written with the appropriate flourish on the title page of the book in front of her.

The flowing handwriting was nothing more than a series of fancy squiggles that had no meaning. She was so thoroughly exhausted that she was beyond being able to recognize even her own name.

She blinked and shook her head slightly, striving to concentrate. She managed to produce a weak but passable smile.

"There you are." She handed the thick, hardcover book to the beaming woman standing on the opposite side of the lace-cloth covered table. "I sincerely hope you enjoy *Midnight Embrace.*"

"Oh, I know I will," the woman said, clutching the treasure to her breasts. "I've loved all your books, Miss

Jones-Jenkins. I read them over and over. They're such wonderful stories. So romantic, so touching, so filled with love." She sighed. "Oh, dear, I do go on and on, but I want you to know how much pleasure you've brought into my life with your work."

"That's very kind of you," Jillian said. "I hope I never disappoint you."

The woman moved away and another stepped forward, presenting a book to be autographed. Jillian opened it to the title page, then hesitated, her gaze sweeping over the expanse of the bright, cheerful, well-stocked bookstore.

The man was still there.

He was watching her, she was certain of it.

Jillian, stop it, she admonished herself in the next instant. Tired was tired, but this was a step beyond. If anyone looked at her crooked, or said the slightest cross word, she'd probably burst into hysterical tears like a toddler in need of a nap.

Therefore, she decided, it went without saying that she was overreacting to the presence of the man. He was the only male in the store, and each time she looked in his direction, he was watching her. She was the constant target of his scrutiny, his gaze never seeming to wander from her.

She wrote the name recited by the woman in front of her, then signed her own by rote with the usual flair. Her smile was beginning to feel pasted to her face like a plastic mask.

The man, she mused, as she vaguely heard herself thanking the woman for her loyal support, was extremely handsome. He was about six feet tall, had thick, dark auburn hair, was well tanned, and had just-rugged-enough features. His eyes were brown as best she could tell, but he'd stayed too far away from where she was seated at the table to be certain.

"You want me to write, 'Merry Christmas, Margaret'?" Jillian asked the next patron. "But this is only February."

"I know, dear." The woman smiled. "I'm shopping early for the holidays in December. That way I feel Christmassy all year long."

"Oh, I see," Jillian said, with a mental shrug.

Whatever floats your boat...dear, she tacked on in her mind. Now where was she in her mental inventory of the tall, handsome stranger skulking in the aisles?

Oh, yes...he was in his early thirties. His nice build was shown to advantage in expensive charcoal-gray slacks and a black V-neck sweater over a white dress shirt worn open at the neck. It was appropriate apparel for Ventura, California, at this time of year.

"I hope Margaret likes the book when she reads it next Christmas," she said.

"Oh, I'm sure she will," the woman said. "Of course, *I'll* read it now. I wouldn't dream of waiting that long for one of your stories."

Jillian laughed. "Happy February to you, and Merry Christmas to Margaret."

"Oh, aren't you a sweet girl?" the woman said. "It was so delightful to meet you, dear." She hurried away.

Delightful? Jillian thought. No, delightful would be a long bubble bath, with soft music playing on the stereo. Then she would slip between crisp sheets on her bed, burrow into the pillow, snuggle beneath the blankets, and sleep, sleep, sleep. Now *that* scenario was delightful.

Deedee Hamilton, the attractive woman in her early thirties who owned Books and Books, stepped closer to the table.

"Let's keep the line moving, please, ladies," she said pleasantly. "It's getting late, and we don't want to detain Miss Jones-Jenkins past regular store hours. She has just returned from an exhausting ten-city book-signing tour, and was good enough to come here before she went home and collapsed. So, let's hurry right along, shall we? Next?"

Bless you, Deedee, you're a wonderful friend, Jillian thought, accepting the book the next woman handed her. Jillian Jones-Jenkins was tired to the point of being numb. Jillian Jones-Jenkins was— Good grief, she was thinking of herself in the abstract, as though she were a character in one of her books. She desperately needed to crawl into bed and not reappear for at least twenty-four hours.

Ten minutes later, Deedee once again came to the table.

"I'm going to close the store now," she announced to the remaining customers. "I'll unlock the door and let each of you out after you've had your book autographed. If any of you are making other purchases as well, please step up to the register."

Ah-ha, Jillian thought, it was truth time. The man— the Handsome Hunk, aka H.H.—was going to have to put up or shut up. His skulking-in-the-aisles routine had just been called to a halt by Deedee.

Jillian inwardly sobered, although her forced smile remained in place.

She should not be taking the presence of the loitering man so lightly. She had writer friends who had been bothered and actually frightened by mentally off-balance men convinced that a woman who wrote love scenes was automatically available to participate in real sexual encounters. Because she was exhausted to the point of being giddy, she hadn't given the man serious enough attention. There was a reason for his having been in the store for such a long time, wandering around, and *watching her*. She was going on red alert as of that very moment.

She glanced up, only to realize that the man had moved again. A visual sweep of the store found him in the cookbook section, his nose in an open cookbook. *Oh, dear heaven, it was upside down!*

A shiver coursed through Jillian, and her smile slid off her chin, despite her efforts to keep it firmly in place. She handed the book she had just signed to the smiling woman, who grasped it eagerly. Only one more customer waited to have a book autographed.

One more, Jillian thought, then the man was going to have to do something. But what? *Oh, Lord, what was he going to do?*

This was it, Forrest MacAllister thought. Time had run out. He had to do it *now*.

He glanced at the cookbook he was holding, then did a quick double take as he realized that he was holding it upside down. Slamming it shut, he shoved it back onto the shelf.

Get it together, MacAllister, he told himself firmly. The situation was as good as it was going to get. The witnesses were pared down to the minimum. He had to do what he'd come here to do—have Andrea's copy of Jillian's novel autographed.

Jillian Jones-Jenkins was certainly attractive. The spokeswoman for the store, who was probably Deedee Hamilton, had confirmed what Andrea had told him yesterday—Miss Jones-Jenkins had just returned from an exhausting book-signing tour. Well, if that was what the

lovely author looked like totally exhausted, she'd be unbelievable when fully rested.

Yes, Forrest decided, she was stunning, tired or not.
Her wavy, dark brown hair fell gently to just above her
shoulders. She had delicate features, sensual lips, and
big, gorgeous, gray eyes framed by long black lashes.
Those eyes were fantastic.

At one point during his vigil she'd stood, apparently to
relax stiff muscles, and he'd had a delightful view of a
slender, yet ultrafeminine figure shown to perfection in
a dusty rose suit with a straight skirt, thigh-length jacket,
and pale pink silky blouse. She was fairly tall, maybe
five-six or -seven, and was, he guessed, about thirty years
old.

All in all, Forrest mentally rambled on, she was a
lovely representative of the female species.

He sighed.

What Jillian Jones-Jenkins did, or did not, look like
had nothing whatsoever to do with why he was there, or
the fact that he couldn't stall any longer.

Then there was the nagging problem that Andrea,
nutsy little sister that she was, wanted him to take on Jillian Jones-Jenkins as an Angels and Elves assignment.
Andrea definitely had too much time on her hands. Her
idea was crazy, totally bizarre.

He'd get the book signed by Miss She-needed-to-
lighten-up-and-have-some-fun Jillian, deliver it to his
sister, and tell her in no uncertain terms that her request
was hereby rejected and his answer was an irrevocable no.

"Thank you so much," Jillian said, handing over the
signed book. "I hope you enjoy it."

"I'm sure I will," the woman said. "Thank you, Miss
Jones-Jenkins. I can't begin to tell you how exciting it
was to meet you."

"Good night, and come again," Deedee said. She unlocked the door and the woman said goodbye with an added promise to shop there often. "Christy," Deedee said to the teenager behind the cash register, "off you go. You did splendidly under the gun. That was really quite a crowd we had in here."

Gun? Jillian thought, swallowing a near-hysterical bubble of laughter. Deedee could have gone all week without saying the word *gun*. Oh, Lord, the man with the gun, who read cookbooks upside down, was starting toward her. He was stalking. Yes, perfect word. He had a smooth, athletic gait that was like a panther *stalking* his prey.

And *she* was the prey.

And *he* had a gun.

No, no. Wait. She had to calm down. The man didn't have a gun. Well, not that she knew of, anyway. Her exhausted brain had simply transferred Deedee's innocently spoken word into a sinister plot. No, there was *not* a gun. Was there?

He was getting closer, she thought, feeling another shiver whisper down her spine. His eyes really were brown. Beautiful eyes. In fact, he was an all-around beautiful man. What a shame that he was a sex maniac, who was about to kidnap her and . . .

Jillian jumped to her feet and grabbed the only weapon available to her—the pen she'd been using to autograph the books.

"Stay back!" she yelled, thrusting the pen toward him. "You come one step closer, you fiend, and I'll . . . I'll ink you to death!"

Forrest stopped dead in his tracks, his eyes widening in shock.

"Pardon me?" he said.

"Jillian?" Deedee called out. She finished locking the door after an exiting Christy, then went to Jillian's side. "What's wrong?"

"This . . . this villain has been skulking in the aisles for over two hours."

"Villain?" Forrest repeated, raising his eyebrows. "Skulking?"

"Don't you move." Jillian whipped the pen back and forth. "Deedee, call the police. Quickly. Go to the telephone and—"

"Hey, now wait a minute," Forrest said.

"Jillian," Deedee said, "sweetie, you're so tired you're not thinking clearly. I'm certain that Mr.—?" She raised her eyebrows questioningly as she looked at him.

"MacAllister," he answered quickly. "Forrest MacAllister, but feel free to call me Forrest."

"Right," Jillian said, with a very unladylike snort of disgust. "You probably made up that name the very second Deedee asked you, you miscreant."

"Miscreant?" Forrest said. He looked at Deedee with a frown. "Does she always talk like this? 'Villain? Skulking? Miscreant?'"

Deedee shrugged. "She writes historical novels. The jargon of the era sort of . . . well, sticks to her at times, especially when she's exhausted or stressed."

"Oh," he said, nodding. "Fascinating."

"Deedee!" Jillian shrieked. "Would you please call the police?"

"Calm down, Jillian," Deedee said gently. "Let's listen to Mr. MacAllister, Forrest's, explanation of why he was 'skulking,' shall we?"

"Would you stop being so condescending?" Jillian said, through clenched teeth. "You're treating me as though I'm a four-year-old throwing a tantrum."

"Then quit acting like one," Forrest said, glowering at her.

"Well!" Jillian said indignantly. "You're not only a cad, you're a rude cad to boot."

"Cad?" He rolled his eyes heavenward. "I don't believe this. A rude cad." He burst into laughter, then grinned at Jillian. "You're really something." She was enchanting, absolutely delightful, as well as being extremely beautiful. "I've always had a fondness for the old-fashioned. You, however, take that premise beyond the scope of my imagination. You're an intriguing woman, Miss Jones-Jenkins." His smile faded, and he looked directly into her eyes. "Yes, very intriguing."

Jillian opened her mouth to retort, then snapped it shut as she realized she had no idea what to say. A tingling sensation danced along her spine and across her breasts before settling low within her. The warm, brown pools of Forrest MacAllister's eyes seemed to be holding her immobile, unable to think clearly, hardly able to breathe.

Dear heaven, she thought hazily, what was this man doing to her?

Not a thing, she mentally answered herself in the next instant. He was just a man, nothing fancy. He put his pants on one leg at time, just like any other man.

Actually, it wasn't a good idea to be focusing on the subject of Mr. MacAllister's pants, Jillian admonished herself.

But, good gracious, he was gorgeous. There was a blatant masculinity about him, an earthy aura that shouted the fact that he was male. Dear heaven, was he ever male. And those eyes, those pinning-her-in-place brown eyes were—

Jillian, stop, stop, stop! she scolded herself. She was overreacting to everything because she was exhausted. She'd had enough of this nonsense.

She tore her gaze from Forrest's, and dropped the pen onto the table.

"Oh, perdition," she said, throwing up her hands. "This is ridiculous. Just what exactly is it that you want, Mr. MacAllister?"

You, Forrest thought. Jillian's big gray eyes were incredible. He felt as though he were being pulled into their fathomless depths, into a sensual fog that caused heat to rocket through his body and coil low and tight within him.

She was a spell weaver. Miss Jillian Jones-Jenkins talked like she had stepped out of the past and into his present. She was rattling him, throwing him off kilter. Well, hell—and perdition, too, for crying out loud.

"Hello?" Deedee said. "Has a truce been called? Is anyone still awake here?"

"I'm not a miscreant," Forrest said, shaking his head. "Okay? Are we clear on that one? I'm here for a purpose."

"Do tell," Jillian said, crossing her arms over her breasts.

"I'm attempting to do that, madam," he said, glaring at her. "I bought one of your books when I first came in. It's behind the counter and has my name on it."

"So, why were you skulking?" Jillian asked, leaning toward him slightly. "Answer me that."

"Because the book is for my sister, Andrea," he said, his voice rising. "Andrea MacAllister Stewart? Your friend? You know, the one who's expecting twins and has been instructed by her doctor to stay in bed because they don't want the babies to be born too early. She's very disappointed that she couldn't come here today."

"Of course," Deedee said, beaming, "Forrest MacAllister. Andrea has spoken of you so often, and was very excited that you were coming home from Japan. And, my, my, here you are. Isn't this a marvelous surprise, Jillian? We're finally meeting Andrea's brother, Forrest."

"Mmm." Jillian lifted her chin a notch. "Being Andrea's brother does not explain Mr. MacAllister's lengthy stretch of skulking."

"Well, hell, what do you expect?" he said, volume now on high. "Do you think I was going to stand in line with a bunch of giggling, fawning women to have a sappy romance novel autographed? Not in this lifetime, sweetheart."

"Uh-oh," Deedee muttered.

Uh-oh, Forrest thought, *that* had not been a brilliant thing to say.

Fury was building in Jillian like a tempestuous storm, gaining force, soon ready to explode. Eyes that had been radiating gray, pussy willow softness, were now silver daggers prepared to strike him dead. The flush on her cheeks was caused by anger, and her breasts, those full, lush breasts, rapidly rose and fell in an enticing rhythm.

She was absolutely sensational.

"You...you..." Jillian sputtered.

"Wait, whoa, halt," Forrest said. He quickly raised both hands in a gesture of peace. "That didn't sound right. What I meant to say is..." *Think, MacAllister!* He was a breath away from being murdered! "A man, any man, is out of his league in a large group of women. It's overwhelming, you know what I mean?" He produced his most dazzling smile. "I was nervous, shaking in my shorts."

"Like hell," Jillian said, narrowing her eyes.

Forrest's smile disappeared. "I don't think they said that back in the old-fashioned days. Anyway, I'm sure your book is great, really wonderful. I like romance. Hell, I love romance. I'm a very romantic guy. Really. You can ask any woman I've ever— Cancel that."

"Mr. MacAllister," Jillian said.

"Forrest. Call me Forrest. Look, I'm in awe of anyone who can write a book and get it published. All I can do in the writing arena is make out checks to pay my bills. I'd appreciate it if you'd autograph the copy of your book I bought for Andrea. Having your newest novel to read will help take her mind off her worries about the babies.

"Listen, I'll read the book myself, cover to cover. I'm sorry if I insulted you. I stressed out because of all those women, that's all. Would you please sign the book for Andrea?"

Oh, perdition, Jillian thought, Forrest MacAllister didn't play fair. There had been an endearing, little-boy quality about him as he spilled forth his sermonette.

Also evident was a genuine sincerity in his voice, and she knew without doubt that he loved his sister, Andrea, very deeply.

Ever since she and Andrea had become friends, Jillian had been aware that the MacAllisters were a close-knit, devoted-to-each-other family. When she was growing up she used to daydream, to fantasize, about how wonderful it would be to have brothers and sisters, and parents who—

"Jillian?" Forrest said.

"Yes, of course," she said, smiling. "I'll be happy to autograph Andrea's book."

"Praise the Lord," Deedee said, looking heavenward. She hurried to retrieve the book from behind the counter, then shoved it into Jillian's hands. "Write."

Jillian sat down behind the table and did as instructed. A few minutes later, she held out the book to Forrest.

"There you are," she said. "I hope Andrea enjoys it. Please tell her that I'll come visit her very soon."

"Thank you," he said, taking the novel from her hand. "Thank you very much."

Again their eyes met, and again neither moved, nor hardly breathed. Currents of crackling sensuality seemed to weave back and forth between them, drawing them close even while they stayed exactly where they were. Their hearts raced, and heat pulsed within as their startling passion heightened.

"Well, I . . ." Deedee started.

"What!" Jillian and Forrest both jerked in surprise at the sound of Deedee's voice and the spell was broken.

Placing one hand over her heart, Deedee said, "All I was going to say is that we're finished here, and you can head for home and collapse, Jillian. I wish I could drive you, but I'm due at a Women in Business meeting."

"I'll call a taxi," Jillian said, getting to her feet. "Don't give it another thought, Deedee."

"I'd be happy to take you home, Miss . . ." Forrest paused. "Jillian."

"Oh, no, a taxi will be fine, Mr. MacAllister. Thank you," she said, not looking at him.

"Forrest. Please accept my offer of a ride. It will help make up for my frightening you while I was 'skulking.' At least I now know that I can 'skulk' in case the need for it ever arises. I'll drive you home. Right? Right. That's settled. Let's go."

"Good idea," Deedee said. "There's nothing to worry about, Jillian. We know Andrea, Forrest is Andrea's brother, and that's good enough for me. It's fine with you, too, but you're too tired to realize it."

"But—" Jillian began, but no one paid any attention to her.

"Jillian came here right from the airport," Deedee informed Forrest. "Her luggage is in the back room. I'll let you out the front door so you can get your car. Drive down the alley to the rear entrance and we'll load you up."

"But—" Jillian tried again.

"Got it," Forrest said, starting toward the front door. Deedee was right behind him.

"Fine," Jillian said, throwing up her hands. "Whatever."

Once the rear door of the store was locked behind Jillian and Forrest, Deedee hurried to the telephone and called Andrea.

"It was touch and go, Andrea," Deedee said breathlessly, "but I did it. Forrest is, as we speak, driving Jillian home. Goodness, your brother is a dreamboat. Anyway, so far, so good...well, providing Jillian doesn't murder him before they get to her house. Now then, tomorrow I'll..."

Two

Forrest's car was a late-model silver BMW sedan with a plush, gray interior. Jillian settled onto the seat with a weary sigh of pleasure, inhaling the heavenly aroma of rich leather in the process.

Sleep, she thought. It was a twenty-minute drive to her house, and then she could sleep, sleep, sleep. And during said drive, she would not pay one iota of attention to Mr. Forrest MacAllister.

The man was a menace. His blatant masculinity had a disturbing effect on her, making her acutely aware of her own femininity. She had felt it—desire—heated and pulsing deep and low within her. Oh, yes, that had been desire; very *unwelcome* desire.

Big macho deal, she thought, leaning her head back and closing her eyes. It didn't mean a thing. It had all been a product of her bone-weary fatigue. Forrest was driving her home, she would bid him adieu, and that would be that. She'd never see him again.

Never? Never again gaze into those incredible chocolate-brown eyes? Never again imagine what it might be like to sink her fingers into the thick depths of his auburn hair? Never again see his sensual lips, his rugged, handsome face, the wide, solid width of his shoulders? Never again hear the rich timbre of his laughter? Never again...

Oh, Jillian, please. Just shut up. Think about sleep, and shut up.

She blanked her mind and drifted off into a light slumber.

Beautiful, Forrest thought, glancing over at her. He quickly redirected his attention to the heavy rush-hour traffic. He was certain Jillian was asleep. Her breathing was slow and steady, her delicate features relaxed and lovely.

It would be nice to think that she was so comfortable in his presence, and trusted him enough, that she could allow herself to doze off. Nice, but not true. She was exhausted, and would probably have fallen asleep even if he was the miscreant Jack the Ripper.

Perdition, he thought, chuckling softly. He really got a kick out of her bygone-era vocabulary. Jillian Jones-Jenkins was a fascinating woman. Unique. Intelligent. Talented. Compelling. Gorgeous.

But Jillian as one of his Angels and Elves assignments?

Forrest frowned and narrowed his eyes in concentration. He had to think this through in a logical manner.

Getting Jillian to take a fresh look at the structure of her existence, to achieve a healthier balance of work and play, was very important to Andrea and Deedee. That made sense. A concern for another person's well-being was one of the basic ingredients of friendship.

Andrea, due to her extremely pregnant condition, should be spared any kind of stress or upset. Jillian's work habits were causing Andrea stress and upset. If he agreed to take Jillian on as an Angels and Elves assignment, he would be able to remove said stress and upset from Andrea's life.

He certainly hadn't planned to grant Andrea her ridiculous request. No, sir, this was to have been a rare moment in history when his little sister wouldn't get her own way when dealing with big brother Forrest.

But, well, having twins was serious business, and making certain they didn't arrive too early was imperative. He still thought Andrea's idea was ridiculous, and he was absolutely *not* going to be *manipulated* into agreeing to do it.

What he *was* going to do, was ask Jillian to go out on a social basis, and nudge her to reexamine her priorities, because *he* had decided it would be beneficial to Andrea's state of mind. He was being a loyal and loving brother, a true-blue MacAllister.

There, now. He had it all figured out and under control. Andrea might think she'd pushed his buttons again, and that she'd manipulated him into taking this Angels and Elves assignment, but he knew better.

Ah, yes, there were times when a man had to put the needs of others first.

He glanced at Jillian.

Times when he just had to do what he had to do.

Darkness had fallen by the time Forrest reached the address Jillian had given him. He found himself in an affluent neighborhood of large, Spanish-style homes on the edge of Ventura.

As he drove slowly along the circular driveway, motion-sensing security lights came alive, illuminating the entire front of the house.

Forrest glanced over at Jillian to see if the sudden brightness had awakened her, but she slept on. She still didn't stir when he stopped the car and turned off the ignition.

He stared at her for a long moment, resisting the urge to lean across the seat and kiss her inviting and *very* enticing, slightly parted lips. By sheer force of will, he switched his attention to the exterior of the house.

Constructed of white stucco with a red-tile roof, it was one story with tall, narrow windows and an intricately carved, dark wood front door. Low, deep-green shrubbery edged the structure, its vivid color a perfect finishing touch.

Forrest nodded in approval, then turned to look at Jillian again. He tentatively raised one hand, then placed it gently on her shoulder, increasing the pressure of his fingers enough to give her a small shake.

"Jillian?" he said. "You're home. Wake up so you can go to sleep." He frowned; that sounded stupid. "Jillian, yo, Jillian, rise and shine."

"Nay, I say," she mumbled, settling deeper into the seat. "Leave me be."

Forrest grinned, once again enthralled by Jillian's other-era vocabulary.

"Mayhap, Lady Jillian," he said, "it would behoove you to awaken and sally forth to yon hacienda to sleep in your own private chamber." Not bad, MacAllister. He was really getting the hang of this nutsy stuff. "Lady Jillian?"

She slowly lifted her lashes, then a puzzled expression settled over her features.

"What? Where?" She started, then suddenly straightened. "Oh, I..." She looked at Forrest. "I fell asleep. That was extremely rude of me, to say the least. I'm sorry."

"Don't give it another thought. I'm a laid-back taxi driver, and you are one very exhausted passenger."

"I won't argue with you about that," she said, opening the car door. "All I can think about is getting into my bed."

Interesting thought, Forrest mused, as he got out of the car. *More* than interesting.

Jillian went to the front door, yawning as she inserted the key in the lock. Forrest pulled the luggage from the car, managing to tote the four pieces in one trip, and followed Jillian inside to set the suitcases in the entry hall.

He swept his gaze over as much of the interior of the house as he could see. Jillian had decorated with a Southwestern flair in muted tones of salmon, pale turquoise and creamy white, creating a soothing, cool atmosphere.

"Nice," he said, nodding. "Your home is very nice."

"Thank you. I'd give you a tour, but I'm so tired I'd probably get lost." Jillian yawned again. "I'm a total wreck."

"Would you like me to carry forth your luggage to your chamber, Lady Jillian?"

Jillian giggled, then blinked as she realized she'd made the ridiculous sound.

"No, knave," she said, with a flip of one hand. "Leave it be." She smiled. "Thank you for the ride home, Forrest. It was a pleasure meeting you, and I apologize for my odd behavior at the bookstore. When I'm this exhausted, I'm not myself.''

"Well, Miss Whoever-you-are," he said, smiling, "I was wondering if you'd have dinner with me tomorrow night?"

"Dinner? Oh, sure. Fine. Bye.'' She turned and started to walk away.

"Jillian?"

She stopped and looked at Forrest over one shoulder. "Hmm?"

"Don't you think you should lock the door behind me when I leave?"

"Oh. Yes. Of course I should. Perdition, where is my mind?"

"Already in your bed asleep." He went to the door and Jillian shuffled forward to grip the doorknob. "Seven-thirty."

"It is?" she said, appearing confused. "No, it's not that late, is it? Well, maybe it is." She shrugged. "Who cares?"

"No, no, I'll pick you up at seven-thirty tomorrow night for dinner." He paused. "Are you going to remember having this conversation?"

"Of course. No problem."

Forrest took one step back into the house and dropped a quick kiss on her lips.

"Good," he said. "I'll see you then." Excellent. His Angels and Elves assignment was officially launched. "Sleep well, Jillian."

Jillian closed the door slowly, then locked it. The fingertips of one hand floated up to touch her lips. They still tingled from Forrest's kiss.

"Merciful saints," she mumbled. "Oh, Jillian, go to bed."

Ten minutes later, she slipped between the cool sheets on her king-size bed, and was asleep the instant her head met the soft pillow.

At 1:00 a.m., Forrest closed the book he'd been reading since he'd arrived back at his apartment, and stared at the cover.

"'*Midnight Embrace*,'" he read aloud, "'by Jillian Jones-Jenkins.'"

It was an extremely well-written novel. He hadn't expected to enjoy it, but he *had* said he would read it.

To his surprise, he'd become completely engrossed in the intricate plot, found himself cheering on the hero and heroine, and eagerly turning the pages to discover how their dilemma would be solved.

He'd razzed Andrea for years about the sappy romance novels she read. Well, he'd have to eat crow. Bigtime crow, because he intended to ask Andrea if she'd loan him Jillian's other novels so he could read them.

Jillian, he thought, turning the book over to look at the photograph on the back. Lord, she was beautiful. The black-and-white photo didn't do justice to her incredible gray eyes, her silky, dark brown hair, or her peaches-and-cream complexion.

His gaze moved to Jillian's lips.

Oh, yes, those kissable-looking lips were very kissable, indeed. He'd never done anything quite so impulsive and pushy as kissing a woman he'd just met. He hadn't thought about doing it, he'd just suddenly kissed her. And it had been a quick little kiss. No big deal.

Wrong. The moment his lips had touched Jillian's, an explosion of sensations had rocketed through him. He'd wanted to haul her into his arms and deepen the kiss, savor more of her sweet taste, feel her respond to him, woman to man. Heat had thrummed through his body with a nearly staggering intensity.

Miss Jillian Jones-Jenkins had certainly had an impact on him, both physically and mentally. She was endearing and enchanting, with her fatigue-induced old-fashioned vocabulary.

There was a fiery temper there, too, evidenced by her threat to ink him to death with her mighty pen and her volatile reaction to his derogatory remark about romance novels.

Forrest chuckled, placed the book on the table next to him, and got to his feet. He stared down at the glossy photograph.

"Good night, Lady Jillian," he said. "I am definitely, *most definitely,* looking forward to our dinner date."

Well, one thing was beginning to become clear—his Angels and Elves assignment wasn't going to be a study in misery. Spending time with Jillian Jones-Jenkins, helping her get her life back on track with a better balance of labor and leisure, wouldn't be hard to do. Not at all.

He yawned.

"Perdition," he said aloud, "I need some sleep."

Early the next afternoon, Jillian stirred, opened one eye and wondered foggily what hotel she was in. In the next moment, she opened both eyes, smiled, then stretched like a lazy kitten as she realized she was at home.

"Dee-lightful," she said.

But an instant later she frowned, as she became fully awake.

She'd dreamed about Forrest MacAllister. It had been one of those jumbled dreams that made absolutely no sense, and had no real plot, per se; but Forrest had been there, no doubt about it.

He'd been dressed as a member of the English *ton* in the late 1800s, complete with ruffled shirt and frilly cuffs, and thigh-hugging trousers tucked into shining leather boots that came to midcalf. His rich auburn hair had been caught in a queue with a black velvet ribbon.

Jillian narrowed her eyes, concentrating on details of the dream.

She had been decked out in a gorgeous ballgown of green velvet with bows drawing up both front halves of the skirt to reveal a paler-green satin underskirt. The bodice had been cut low to expose just the tops of her breasts, and her hair had been arranged in an elaborate, upswept creation threaded through with narrow green ribbons.

She and Forrest, she realized, had appeared like characters who had stepped from the pages of one of her books. They were the hero and heroine in all their splendor.

That much was clear, but from then on the dream had been a bit wacky. They had been dancing at a crowded ball, swirling gracefully around the floor. In the next moment, though, they'd been waltzing in Deedee's store, and then later in Jillian's own living room.

"Heavens," she said, throwing back the blankets, "what nonsense."

Leaving the bed, she started across the room, only to stop after going a few feet. She placed the fingertips of one hand on her lips, the sudden remembrance of Forrest's quick but unforgettable kiss causing a shiver to skitter along her spine.

Now wait a minute. That kiss had *not* been in the dream. It had taken place in her very own entry hall. That cocky Forrest MacAllister had actually kissed her.

With a cluck of disgust she went into the bathroom, and minutes later was standing under the warm spray of the shower, vigorously shampooing her hair.

In all fairness she had to admit it had been a sensational, albeit short, kiss. And it wasn't as though Forrest had hauled her into his arms and kissed the living daylights out of her—which would have been extremely rude.

No, it had been a rather...polite...yes, polite kiss. A tad pushy, considering they'd only just met, but definitely memorable.

As Jillian dried herself with a huge, fluffy towel, she was aware of a sense of something nagging at her. What was she forgetting? What was vying for attention that she couldn't remember? She had been so exhausted the previous night, there was no telling what she didn't recall in the light of a new day.

With a shrug of dismissal, she left the bathroom and dressed in jeans faded in spots to white, a baggy red sweatshirt that boasted the slogan Writers Always Have the Last Word, and red-and-white polka-dot socks.

After a cup of Earl Grey tea and a bowl of granola and yogurt, she called her secretary, Lorraine, to announce her arrival home.

Ever-efficient Lorraine reported that the necessary bills had been paid during Jillian's absence, the newspaper delivery would resume today, the housekeeper had been instructed to stock the refrigerator yesterday per the usual procedure, and everything was under control.

"You're a gift from the heavens," Jillian said.

"I know," Lorraine said. "I'm fantastic. I have your fan mail here, but fear not, I won't darken your doorway for two weeks. You're officially on vacation as of dawn today. What are you going to do this time?"

"I don't know yet," she said, frowning slightly. "The tour was so hectic I didn't have a spare second to think about it."

"Well, darn," the secretary said. "I look forward to hearing about The Project. That's in capital letters, you understand. Let's see. Over the years, you've used your two-week hiatus to go on a cruise, take knitting lessons, volunteer to read stories to children in the hospital, and on the list goes. My favorite was when you wallpapered the bathroom."

Jillian laughed. "Which had to be redone by a professional."

"True. Goodness, Jillian, it's hard to believe you haven't settled on The Project. This is day one, you know, and you're wasting time even as we speak."

"I realize that. I'm thinking, I'm thinking. I'll talk to you later, Lorraine. Oh, how are your husband and your grandchildren?"

"My darling hubby is still a couch potato, and the grandkids are brilliant and incredibly cute. Bye for now, boss."

Jillian replaced the receiver slowly, then stared at it for a long moment.

Lorraine was right. She'd always decided on The Project well before her coveted two weeks began. Her publisher had her latest book in production, the grueling promotional tour was gratefully over, and she would have her self-indulgent fourteen days before starting a new novel, as per her usual routine.

"Think, Jillian," she told herself.

She thought about The Project while she toted her luggage to her room and unpacked, then stored the suitcases in the back of one of the guest-room closets. She thought while washing and drying clothes, and making a pile to go to the cleaners'. She thought while she sorted through the stack of receipts she'd accumulated during the tour, and made a list of thank-you notes to be written to the bookstore owners who had hosted her autograph parties across the country. She thought while she put the paperwork in her large, sunny office and firmly closed the door, vowing not to open it for fourteen days.

She thought while she ate a peanut-butter and banana sandwich, then watched a talk show on television.

As dusk began to darken the living room, she closed the drapes, turned on several lamps, lit a crackling fire in the hearth, and thought.

She slouched rather ungracefully onto the sofa facing the fireplace, stretching her legs straight out in front of her and wiggling her red-and-white-polka-dot-clad toes. While the wobbling pattern of the socks made her slightly dizzy, it did not transmit a genius-level idea for The Project.

"Food," she said, getting to her feet again. "I'll feed my brain."

A few minutes later, she replaced the receiver of the telephone, having requested a Super Duper Pizza Supreme Deluxe Extraordinaire to be delivered to the house.

Returning to the living room, she began to pace back and forth in front of the fireplace.

"Skydiving?" she muttered. "Oh, good grief, no, I'd probably break myself. Gourmet cooking lessons?" She shook her head. "I'd become fat as a pig. Learn to speak Russian? Japanese? French?" She frowned. "Who would I talk to in Russian? Oh, darn it, I've already wasted one of my precious fourteen days.''

She plopped back onto the sofa with a dejected sigh, and stared gloomily into the nearly-hypnotizing flames of the fire. When the telephone rang, she jerked in surprise as she was startled out of her semitrance. She snatched up the receiver of the telephone on the end table.

''Hello?''

''Jillian? Hi, it's Deedee. I've been trying to call you all day, but it was so busy at the store, I didn't have a chance. There's something important that I need to talk to you about. I'd rather do this in person, but... Do you have time to chat?''

''Sure. What's on your mind?''

''First of all, I want to thank you for doing the autographing yesterday. I know how tired you were, and I appreciate your tacking me onto the end of that grueling tour.''

''No problem. I always enjoy doing book-signings at Books and Books. Your customers are such sweethearts. Now, what's this 'something important' you wanted to talk to me about?''

''Oh, well, you see—'' Deedee paused. ''Since you're speaking to me at the moment, I assume Forrest MacAllister carried out his mission of delivering you safely home. Did you manage to get there without threatening to murder him, or inking him to death?''

''I slept all the way home.''

''Oh, you're such a dud. That is one sexy hunk of man on the hoof, Jillian Jones-Jenkins. He's nice, too. You know how highly Andrea speaks of him. You *slept* all the way home? I'm beginning to think you're hopeless.''

"Me? Look who's talking. You're cruel to the male populace."

"I am not. I'm dating three different men at the moment. It's just that if any of them get too serious, I shoo them out the door."

"You're a coldhearted wench, Deedee. Is this topic the 'something important'?"

"No. Well, yes, sort of. What I mean is—"

"Deedee!"

"Okay, I'm getting it together now." She cleared her throat. "Jillian, I want you to keep an open mind while I'm explaining my 'something important.' Have you settled on The Project for your time off from work yet?"

"No, much to my frustration. I've already wasted an entire day. Why?"

"Well, you see, Andrea is very concerned about Forrest. He worked extremely hard while he was in Japan, with very little time off. He claims he's not going back to work for a few weeks, but Andrea says he'll never do it. He'll end up in the office slaving away.

"She was getting stressed, really having a fit, as we were talking about Forrest. She's so-o-o-o worried about him, Jillian. To calm her down, I suggested we try to think of a way to get him to relax, enjoy his time off, concentrate on something other than work. So, between us we came up with a plan."

"That's all very nice," Jillian said. "However, I'm totally confused as to how this 'something important,' that has turned out to be Forrest's work habits, has anything to do with me."

"Because you're the solution, the answer. Are you ready? Forrest MacAllister will be The Project you'll take on during your vacation."

"What!" Jillian shrieked.

"Jillian, please, just listen. You know Andrea isn't supposed to get stressed right now, but she's doing exactly that over her concerns about Forrest. Andrea needs you, Jillian. You're the only one who can divert Forrest's attention, get him to balance his life better with work and play. I told Andrea I'd talk to you because she gets uptight just discussing her work-weary brother." Deedee sighed. "It's so sad."

"You two are Looney Tunes," Jillian said. "I can't take on Forrest as The Project. He's a person, a human being, a man, for crying out loud. He doesn't qualify for The Project."

"Sure, he does. Whose project is it? Yours. You can do whatever you want to. You just said you hadn't picked anything, and here it is, right before your very eyes. You'd be doing it for your dear friend Andrea, for those adorable twins she's going to have. How can you say no to someone in need like she is? Like Forrest is, for that matter?"

"Deedee, Forrest MacAllister is not the type of man who is lacking in female company."

"Indeed not. But the tricky part is, he doesn't take enough time off to enjoy what's out there. You've got to be brave, courageous and bold. Step right up, invite him out, help him get his life in order. This is a terrific project for you, Jillian. Think how good you'll feel about what you've done for Andrea, and for Forrest."

"No, I'll think about where to get professional help for you and Andrea. You two are not playing with full decks. Deedee, this is crazy."

"It is not! Listen, when the MacAllisters were kids, their mother periodically had them do Angels and Elves assignments. You know, nice things for people—like mowing their lawn, or washing their windows, or whatever. Isn't that the sweetest thing?"

"Too sweet for words," Jillian said, rolling her eyes heavenward.

"So, that's what we're asking you to do here. Forrest MacAllister will be The Project aka your Angels and Elves assignment."

"Deedee..."

"Jillian, don't say no. Just promise me you'll think about it. When you really give this some thought, you'll realize it's perfect. You'll have The Project, Forrest will get his priorities in order, and Andrea will relax and stay calm."

"Deedee, I really don't want—" The doorbell rang, causing Jillian to stop speaking. "Someone is at the door. It must be the pizza I ordered."

"Good. Hang up. Just promise me you'll think about what I proposed."

"Yes, fine, all right, I'll think about it. I've got to go, Deedee. Bye." Jillian dropped the receiver into place and shot to her feet. "Pizza. Brain food." She marched across the living room toward the entry hall. "Andrea and Deedee need some help for *their* brains."

Before opening the door, she grabbed a twenty-dollar bill from the credenza in the entry hall. It was her "cash stash" for the frequent delivery of meals that held more appeal than cooking her own. Flipping on the porch light, even though the motion-sensitive lights would have been activated, she opened the door.

"Hi. That was quick. I only called you a few minutes—" She stopped speaking. Her mouth remained opened as her eyes widened.

Standing before her in the bright light, dressed in a dark gray suit, pale blue shirt, and gray paisley-print tie, looking like he'd just stepped out of the pages of *Gentlemen's Quarterly* magazine, was Forrest MacAllister.

"Andrea?" Deedee said. "We've been momentarily saved by a pizza. Jillian was not going for The Project idea, no way, no how. Then the pizza she ordered was delivered and she had to answer the door. I got her to promise to think about Forrest being The Project.

"Now we wait and see what happens, and keep each other posted if we hear anything. I swear, when we decided that Jillian and Forrest would be perfect for each other, I had no idea that Cupids had to work so hard. This is exhausting. But victory shall be ours! Won't it?"

Three

Forrest MacAllister, Jillian mentally repeated incredulously, was standing in her doorway. Forrest, who had been smiling, but who was now frowning and appearing rather confused as his gaze swept over her attire.

Jillian blinked, cleared her throat, and was unable to hide an expression every bit as confused as his.

"Forrest?" she said. "I thought you were the pizza."

"No," he said slowly, "I'm not a pizza. I'm a man. The one you have a dinner date with."

"I do?"

He nodded. "You do. May I come in?"

"Yes, I think you'd better," she said, stepping back.

Gracious but he was gorgeous. She had a funny little flutter in the pit of her stomach that she couldn't chalk up to hunger. He smelled wonderful, too. His after-shave had a woodsy, very masculine aroma.

As she closed the door, Forrest turned to look at her.

Cute as a button, he thought. Jillian's sweatshirt was baggy, her jeans as old as dirt, and the socks were weird. But she was femininity in spades, causing his heart to increase its tempo.

"I think we've had a communication problem, or something," Jillian said.

"Actually, I was afraid this might happen," he said. "I tried to call you today to confirm our date, but you have an unlisted number."

He could have asked Andrea or Deedee for Jillian's number, he knew, but he wasn't ready to tell either of them that he was taking her out. The cackling glee he would no doubt have been subjected to was something a guy had to gear up for.

"When you agreed to go out with me," he went on, "I wondered if you'd remember."

Jillian splayed one hand on her chest. "*I* agreed to a dinner date for tonight?"

"Yes, ma'am, you did. We were standing right here in your entry hall last night when we made the plans for me to pick you up at seven-thirty."

"Oh, Forrest, I'm so sorry. I don't remember. I *knew* there was something niggling at me, but I couldn't figure out what it was. This is embarrassing, and I sincerely apologize."

"Hey," he said, smiling, "don't worry about it. You were so exhausted that I wasn't certain at the time that you were really tuned in to what we were saying. How about a rain check?"

"Well, I—" she started, then gasped as the doorbell rang again. "Pizza."

She spun around and opened the door. A few minutes later she closed it, and stood holding an enormous, square flat box.

"Mmm," she said, inhaling deeply. "Doesn't that smell delicious?"

"That has got to be the biggest pizza box I've ever seen."

"Isn't it great? It's a Super Duper Pizza Supreme Deluxe Extraordinaire."

Forrest laughed. "That's quite a title."

"Forrest, listen. I feel so badly about not remembering our date. Why don't you stay and share this pizza with me? There's enough here for a regiment of marines. You could take off your jacket and tie, be more comfortable, and we'll have a pizza party."

"Sold."

"Good," she said, matching his smile. "I'm glad."

She really was *very* glad that Forrest had agreed to stay, Jillian mused, as she walked past him into the living room. She hadn't realized that the evening ahead had been looming before her as a series of long, exasperating hours spent attempting to come up with a brilliant idea for The Project.

Oh, dear... The Project, now also known as an Angels and Elves assignment, or mission, or whatever. Forrest MacAllister as The Project? Zero in on his problem of working far too much, get him to relax, have fun? That was nuts, it really was. Wasn't it? She'd promised Deedee that she'd think about the absurd idea, and she'd keep her word. Later.

But now? Forrest was there. She felt suddenly lighthearted and cheerful. Her gloomy mood had completely disappeared. Forrest had been so understanding about her forgetting their date, and he was now going to take part in an impromptu pizza party, despite the fact that he was dressed to the nines.

She was certainly going to erase from her memory bank her first impression of him as being a skulking miscreant. Forrest MacAllister was a very nice man.

Forrest MacAllister was also so drop-dead gorgeous, he was enough to make a woman weep.

"I'll get a tablecloth and spread it on the floor in front of the fireplace," Jillian said. "That will be more fun than eating in the kitchen. I'll be right back."

Forrest pulled off his tie as he watched Jillian leave the room.

A pizza picnic, he thought. Jillian Jones-Jenkins was really something. When he'd first seen her at Books and Books, she'd appeared every bit the professional career woman. Who would have guessed that she was the type to wear polka-dot socks and eat pizza while sitting on the floor?

An intriguing woman was Lady Jillian, with many layers to be discovered, like unwrapping a Christmas present. He'd been looking forward to taking her to a classy restaurant, but the evening ahead definitely held much more appeal. Definitely.

Forrest put his tie in his pocket, removed his jacket and set it on a chair, then slipped off his shoes. He rolled the cuffs of his shirt up a bit, and undid the two top buttons.

He was ready for a pizza picnic, *and* for whatever other delights the evening produced.

Jillian returned with a blue-plaid vinyl tablecloth, which Forrest helped spread out on the floor in front of the fire. She brought in glasses of soda and some napkins, then placed the pizza box in the center of the cloth.

Sitting Indian-style next to each other, their backs against the sofa, they peered into the box when Jillian lifted the lid.

"Holy smoke," Forrest said, laughing. "I hope there isn't going to be a test later on what all that stuff is on that creation."

"It's an exquisite work of art," Jillian said. "Dig in, Forrest."

They ate two slices each, with appreciative "mmms," then slowed a bit on the third.

How strange, Jillian thought, as she took a sip of soda. There was a comfortable, rather peaceful feeling settling over her as she sat on the floor next to Forrest. It felt *right* somehow to have him there, sharing her pizza party.

Yet, at the same time, she was acutely aware of Forrest's masculinity and how it caused her to silently rejoice in her own femininity. Frissons of heat coursed deep within her, awakening her slumbering womanliness. The remembrance of Forrest's quick kiss of the night before was becoming more vivid with each passing moment.

How was it possible, she wondered, to be experiencing such opposite emotions at the same time?

"Jillian," Forrest said, bringing her from her confused thoughts, "I read *Midnight Embrace* last night, and I wanted to tell you that I really enjoyed it."

"Thank you," she said, then took another nibble of pizza.

"I obviously had the wrong impression of what romance novels actually are. When I gave the book to Andrea today, I apologized for having hassled her for years about her choice of reading material."

"That's nice. I hope you aren't missing having anchovies on this pizza. I can't abide those yucky little fish."

"What? Oh, no. I don't like them, either. Anyway, your novel was great. I stayed up late to finish it, because I wanted to find out how the hero and heroine were going to solve their problems. It seemed hopeless there for a while, but you really did a fantastic job of putting the pieces of the puzzle together."

"Thank you. Do you have enough soda?"

"Yes, I'm fine. Do you do your own research? You sure covered the details of clothes, furnishings, food, social graces, the whole nine yards of that era. Do you hire someone to gather that information for you?"

"No, I do my own research. I have an extensive library that encompasses different times in history. Oh-h-h, I'm stuffed. Four slices of pizza is definitely my limit."

"I've had plenty, too. It was delicious, and I thank you for inviting me to share it with you. Was *Midnight Embrace* your choice, or does your editor decide on the title?"

"I titled it *Midnight Embrace*. Sometimes they change what I've chosen for reasons that make absolutely no sense to me."

"Does that bother you?"

"Nope, not anymore. I don't care if the readers remember the title. I want my story, my characters, to stay in their minds. I'll go put the rest of this pizza in the refrigerator."

"Okay." He looked at her thoughtfully. "I'll fold up the tablecloth."

As Jillian busied herself returning things to the kitchen, Forrest tended to the cloth.

Interesting, he mused. He was getting the distinct impression that Jillian didn't want to talk about her work. He'd assumed that someone with her level of talent would enjoy discussing writing with anyone who showed a flicker of interest. But not Jillian Jones-Jenkins.

He'd dated women who were so involved in their careers they couldn't be bothered to chat about the weather, or anything else, for that matter. Jillian's attitude had caught him off guard, but it was very refreshing.

The confusing part was that Andrea and Deedee were concerned that Jillian was *too* focused on her work. If that was true, then why didn't she want to discuss it? Maybe writers had eccentric superstitions or something, that dictated that they save their mental energies for the actual creative process, and not waste any by talking about their craft. Yes? No? He really didn't know.

Jillian came back into the room, scooped up the tablecloth, then headed for the kitchen again.

Forrest was fascinated by the fact that she was a writer, she mused. Most people she met for the first time found her career intriguing. She usually enjoyed answering all their questions—even while on vacation—as it was easy to talk about something she loved so dearly.

Tonight, however, she needed to direct the conversation to center on Forrest. If, and that was a very big if, she decided to make Forrest The Project, she had to know more about him, what made him tick, determine why he worked harder than was necessary.

Jillian returned to the living room and sat down next to Forrest again. At the same moment, they both shifted slightly to be able to look directly at each other. Their eyes met, and neither spoke.

Lord, Forrest thought, Jillian's eyes were incredible. He'd never seen eyes that gray, eyes that reminded him of a London fog, of a soft, fuzzy kitten. Would they change color when she was consumed with desire, when passion reigned? He wanted to know. He wanted to make love with Jillian Jones-Jenkins.

Jillian tore her gaze from Forrest's and picked an imaginary thread from her sweatshirt.

How much time had passed since she'd looked directly into Forrest's chocolate-brown eyes? She honestly didn't know. She'd been pinned in place, with the sudden rapid tempo of her heartbeat echoing in her ears.

Forrest MacAllister was dangerous because he was exciting, evoking undeniable desire within her, and causing her mind to travel down a road that she had no intention of taking.

"So," she said, a tad too loudly. She looked at Forrest's chin. "Andrea has told me that you're a family of architects. She said your father started the firm years ago on a shoestring and a dream, with your mother as his secretary. Now you're all involved in the company."

"Yep, we're MacAllister Architects, Incorporated. Our folks are retired now, and are having a fabulous time traveling here, there and everywhere. My brother Ryan isn't an architect. He's a police officer, a very dedicated cop."

"I don't remember who is the oldest brother."

"Michael. He's married and has a son. Great kid. Michael likes the challenge of taking on remodeling projects. He's done a lot of plans for restoration work, and is beginning to have more jobs than he can handle. Ryan is next in line as far as age. He got married about three months ago. Andrea is the baby of the family."

"Did you hire someone to take Andrea's place now that she's been ordered to stay in bed?"

Forrest nodded. "Andrea hired a sharp gal. You see, not only is Andrea an architect, she also has a bachelor's degree in landscape architecture. Most people don't realize that landscaping can be that complicated, so as to require a college degree.

"Because of Andrea, we're a full-service firm. In other words, we can design a home *and* the landscaping to enhance it, if the client wishes. We're really proud of Andrea. And we miss her now that she's concentrating on her family."

Jillian smiled and met Forrest's gaze again. "It's very obvious that you're all very close. That's nice, really lovely."

"It's always been that way." He shrugged. "It can be a pain in the rear, because family members don't hesitate to give their opinion on what you're doing, whether you've asked for it or not. But the majority of the time it's good to know they're all there."

"It sounds wonderful. I'm an only child, who grew up wishing I had brothers and sisters, and parents who— Well, brothers and sisters."

Parents who what? Forrest wondered. What had Jillian been about to say?

"I think I have everyone in your family straight now," she said.

It was nitty-gritty, fact-finding time. She'd become very adept over the years at phrasing her questions in a manner that provided her with the information she wanted to know. She was about to do her thing, just in case she decided to make Forrest The Project, which she probably wouldn't, but . . . well, just in case.

"That leaves you," she said, smiling. "You're what? About thirty?"

"Thirty-two."

"I had my thirtieth birthday a few months ago. From what everyone said, I was expecting a black depression to settle over me." She shrugged. "It didn't happen."

"Well, I guess some people feel if you're not married by thirty, you're doomed."

"I was married at twenty, divorced at twenty-two. Now *that* was a doomed relationship."

"What happened?"

"It's old news," she said, waving one hand breezily in the air. "It's not worth talking about. We're discussing you. You're the only one in your family who isn't married." She laughed. "If you *are* married, I'm going to be very peeved that you had the nerve to eat my pizza."

Forrest raised one hand in the air and placed the other over his heart.

"I am not," he said, with a mock-serious expression on his face, "nor have I ever been, married, ma'am."

"Yes, I know. I was only kidding. Andrea mentioned that you weren't married. But—" she leaned slightly toward him "—why not?"

"I haven't found the right woman." Heaven knew, he'd been looking, but wherever she was hiding, she was doing a hell of a good job of it. "It's as simple as that."

Bingo, Jillian thought. Men had no imagination whatsoever. They should hold a mass meeting and come up with fresh material. She'd heard that line countless times. It was the pat answer—a cliché due to overuse— and easily understood by single women across the country: *Forrest was not interested in marriage.*

Yep, she thought, the "I haven't found the right woman" guys were varying degrees of playboys. No serious commitments for that bunch. No, sir.

"I imagine," she said, adopting a casual tone of voice, "that your house and the landscaping must look like something out of a magazine, considering what you, Andrea and Michael do for a living."

"I don't have a house," he said. He'd once believed that he would. Oh, yeah, a big, sprawling place that would echo with children's laughter. There would be a huge backyard to play in, with plenty of room for kids and a dog. Maybe a cat, too. "I live in a high-rise apartment."

Ah-ha, Jillian thought. Apartment, not a house. *Forrest wanted no part of mowing the lawn, fixing drippy faucets, lugging trash cans to the curb and back. There wasn't a domestic bone in his body.*

She looked at her socks, wiggling her toes and watching the polka dots dance a jig.

"I was thinking about Andrea and John," she said. "Twins. Your entire family must be excited. Twins are so cute."

Forrest laughed. "Twins are an overwhelming thought." Double the joy, as well as the work. "Two of everything, that's what Andrea and John are getting into. Whew."

"That's for sure," she said, nodding. "I'm reading you loud and clear." *Forrest MacAllister wasn't crazy about babies, or the idea of being a father.*

Well done, Jillian, she mentally praised herself. She'd collected the data and computed it. Forrest was an upwardly mobile, swinging single, entertaining absolutely no plans for marriage, hearth, home or child.

"Please don't misunderstand what I'm saying here, Jillian," Forrest said. "I *want* to get married, have kids, a home."

Jillian's eyes widened. "You do? But you said . . . I mean . . . You do?"

"Yes, I truly do. I guess I'm gun-shy because I've seen so many of my friends end up getting divorced. The basic problem appears to be that in two-career marriages there just isn't enough time to be a real family. The careers always seem to take first place."

"Oh," Jillian said. Could she really be that far off base on the conclusions she'd drawn? She'd never been so completely wrong before. Maybe Forrest MacAllister wasn't run-of-the-mill after all. "Well, there is a little thing known as compromise, Forrest."

He frowned. "They don't work that often. Oh, it starts out fine, but more and more of the people I know run into trouble. Hey, I'm not a chauvinist who feels a woman belongs in the home being a wife and mother, and shouldn't have a career. I'm just coming to the conclusion that the life-style a two-career marriage produces isn't what I want.

"I'm destined, I guess, to being a bachelor, and satisfying my paternal instincts by interacting with my nieces and nephews."

"Ah, I see," Jillian said thoughtfully. "So you engage in casual dating, and focus the remainder of your energy on your job."

He shrugged. "I enjoy my work. I get a lot of satisfaction out of the ongoing challenge of it."

"Hmm," Jillian said, staring into space.

No wonder Andrea was worried about Forrest. The man had an attitude problem. He'd obviously done some data gathering of his own and had drawn harsh conclusions from the information. But despite what he believed, two-career marriages *could* be happy, fulfilling, and everything Forrest was wistfully wishing for.

She herself wanted no part of being married. Not ever again! But she sincerely believed that those who did want that life-style could create a marvelous union—two careers included—if they shared, and cared, and compromised. Forrest was burying his hopes and dreams in an overload of work, instead of being determined to have what he wanted.

Not good. This man needed help, had to be shown the errors in his thinking. He was sentencing himself to a lonely life, and that was incredibly sad. He just worked, worked, worked, to fill the void in his existence. *Her* heavy work schedule suited her perfectly. Forrest's did not serve him well.

There was no hope for it; she was hooked. She would take Forrest on, reprogram his poor, malfunctioning brain on the subject of marriage and dual careers.

For starters she'd get him to lighten up on his own work schedule to demonstrate how compromise in that area could be accomplished.

As crazy as it was, Forrest MacAllister was now officially The Project, her Angels and Elves assignment as Deedee called it.

"Jillian?" Forrest said, bringing her back to attention. "Is it all right if I put another log on the fire? It's burning pretty low."

Jillian nodded, then watched absently as he began to tend to the chore. Within moments, her casual observation became red-alert awareness, missing no detail of him performing the task at hand.

He had shifted to hunker down in front of the fireplace, balancing on the balls of his feet as only a person with athletic control of his body was capable of doing.

His shirt strained across his broad shoulders as he reached for a log, and was tucked into slacks that defined a narrow waist. There were powerful muscles in his legs, outlined to perfection beneath his expensive slacks. She also had the enticing view of an extremely nice male tush to scrutinize.

The flush on her cheeks and the heat that was swirling within her was not, she knew, caused by the flames in the hearth.

Forrest MacAllister was throwing her off kilter again by the male magnetism emanating from him. She'd have to be on guard against his blatant sexuality during The Project. She didn't intend to go to bed with the man, for heaven's sake; casual sex was not in her plan.

But since she knew that she was easily unsettled by Forrest's masculine appeal, she was one step ahead of things, in total control of herself.

The Project, aka her Angels and Elves assignment, was officially launched.

"There we go," Forrest said, moving back against the couch.

He sat closer to Jillian this time, his shoulder pressed to hers.

Oh, yes, she mused, the prospect of two weeks with Forrest was certainly better than taking knitting lessons. Much, *much* better.

Four

The next two hours flew by, as Jillian and Forrest chatted, never running out of topics to discuss as one subject flowed into the next.

"Tell me about Japan," Jillian said.

"It was fantastic," he said. "Even though I was working seven days a week, I managed to see at least some of the sights. Japan has such grace and elegance."

"My, what a lovely way to describe it."

"Well, it's true. And the people? They're wonderful. I swear, Jillian, the kids steal your heart in a second. I was invited to a birthday party and the children were dressed in authentic Japanese clothing. Cute? Oh, man, they were like walking, talking dolls.

"I took so many pictures of them, they'll probably remember me as the tall guy with a camera for a face. I wanted to scoop them all up and bring them home."

What a wonderful father Forrest would be, Jillian mused. His expressive brown eyes were shining as he spoke of the children he'd seen in Japan. He should have a family of his own, he really should.

"Enough about me," he said. "How long does it take you to write a book?"

"Several months. I hardly come up for air when I'm on a deadline."

There it was, Forrest thought, the first hint of Jillian's working hard; *too* hard, according to Andrea and Deedee.

"Couldn't you ask for more time from your publisher so you *could* come up for air?"

Jillian shrugged. "The schedule I'm on suits me just fine."

Andrea and Deedee were right, Forrest decided. This lady needed to be taken in hand, shown how to interweave work and play into her existence. Nice guy that he was, he was going to teach her how to do exactly that.

She believed in the premise of compromises in a two-career relationship. *Those* compromises were rarely successful, but Jillian could compromise with *herself* and have a better balance.

Forrest was pulled from his thoughts as Jillian urged him to relate more delightful tales of growing up with two brothers and a mischievous little sister. As he concluded yet another story, she laughed so hard she had to wrap her arms around her stomach.

What an enchanting sound, Forrest mused, a wide smile on his face. Jillian's laughter was like tinkling bells, like wind chimes. Her gray eyes were sparkling with merriment, and her smile was real and beautiful.

"Oh, dear," Jillian said, catching her breath. "I hope I don't get the hiccups from laughing. That happens sometimes. Your parents must have the patience of saints to have raised the four of you.''

"Either that, or they went numb at some point," he said, chuckling. "We were a handful, all right." He paused. "Tell me about *your* parents, Jillian."

Her smile faded. "There's not much to tell. My father is a foreign diplomat, an ambassador. He's excellent at what he does, and was kept on through the years when the political administrations changed. We lived in England, Mexico, France, you name it. They're in Italy now."

"That's a remarkable childhood. It sounds very exciting."

"It wasn't," she said quietly. "Being a foreign diplomat is a very social existence. My mother is devoted to my father and his career, and I admire and respect that. But I was left in the care of a nanny, or housekeeper, or whatever, the majority of the time.

"I have vivid memories of my parents coming to the nursery to kiss me good-night, but there were no hugs because they'd didn't want to wrinkle their evening clothes.''

"You were lonely," Forrest said, in the form of a statement, not a question.

"Yes. They sent me to the United States for high school. I went to a fancy boarding school in upper New York State, then on to Stanford. When I became a published author, which was my dream, I immediately began to save my money to buy a house so that I could stay put, not have to move from place to place."

"You have a lovely home."

"Thank you. I like it, and I'm very contented here. I... Goodness, listen to me. I can't remember when I've talked about my childhood. I certainly sounded sorry for myself. It wasn't all that bad. My folks are wonderful people, and I know they love me. They simply didn't have much time for me."

Forrest frowned. "I'm sorry."

"Heavens," she said, forcing a smile, "don't be. It's because of being alone so much as a child that I was able to achieve my goal in writing. I used to make up stories by the hour to entertain myself. I developed my imagination to its maximum potential. And, ta-da, I'm an author."

"A very talented author. Is your father Ambassador Jones, or Ambassador Jenkins?"

"Jones. I took back my maiden name after my divorce, but when I sold my first book, my agent urged me to add my married name of Jenkins. She felt that Jillian Jones-Jenkins had a better ring to it than just Jillian Jones. And that, sir, is the story of my life. Dull."

"Not even close." He looked directly into her eyes. "And your marriage?"

"Was a mistake. Like I said before, that's old news, and not worth discussing." She cocked her head slightly to one side. "You know, Forrest, you're a wonderful listener. I'm a very private person, despite my having to be in the limelight at times to further my career. I could count on one hand the number of people I've told about my childhood, yet I dumped it all on you."

"Shared, not dumped, and I'm honored," he said. "I sincerely am." He cradled her cheek with one hand, and moved his head slowly toward hers. "Very—" he brushed his lips over hers "—very—" his other hand lifted to frame her face "—honored."

His lips captured hers, parting them, his tongue delving into her mouth.

Jillian's eyes drifted closed, and her hands floated upward to grip Forrest's shoulders. A tremor swept through her, then heat that swirled low and steady within her.

Her senses were heightened as she savored the taste of Forrest, the feel of his work-roughened hands on the soft skin of her face, his aroma of woodsy after-shave, mesquite smoke from the fire, and soap.

She was awash with consuming desire, her breasts suddenly yearning for a soothing caress. She met Forrest's tongue boldly; dueling, dancing, stroking with a rhythm that matched the heated pulse in the dark center of her femininity.

She couldn't think, she could only feel.

And it was ecstasy.

Jillian, Forrest's mind thundered. The kiss had begun as one of comfort, meant to ease the pain of her lonely childhood. He could picture her in his mind's eye as a little girl, creating characters in stories as playmates because there was no one else to keep her company. His heart ached for her as he envisioned the cold emptiness of her youth. He had willed the memories to fade, had wished to bring her back to the present, with him.

And so, he'd kissed her.

But now? Dear Lord, he was at the edge of his control, flung there the moment his lips had claimed hers. He wanted to make love to her. It was a burning need, an intensity like nothing he'd experienced before.

Jillian Jones-Jenkins.

Her name was a melody, a lilting song that echoed like sweet music in his mind. The mental image of the lonely child had faded into oblivion, replaced by the intriguing, compelling, multilayered woman she was now.

A voice began to sift through his passion-laden haze, coming from a source unknown. It was a message of warning, of caution, telling him to slow down, move carefully, so as not to frighten Jillian away.

Despite her breezy dismissal of her brief marriage, the voice declared, Jillian had been hurt, badly hurt, in the past. Why he knew that, he didn't know. Where the voice was coming from was a mystery.

What *was* crystal clear was that he mustn't do anything to cause her to refuse to see him again. Jillian was his Angels and Elves assignment. In his hazy state he'd completely forgotten that she was more than just an enchanting woman.

Mustering his last ounce of willpower, he broke the kiss, then slowly, reluctantly, dropped his hands from her face.

Jillian opened her eyes, and Forrest stifled a groan at the smoky hue of her gray eyes that mirrored the desire in his own.

"Jillian?" he said, hearing the desire-induced rasp of his voice.

"Hmm?" she murmured dreamily. A soft smile formed on her lips. "Yes, Forrest?"

"We'd better cool off here, don't you think? I want to make love with you, believe me, I really do, but . . ."

"You're right," she said, then took a wobbly breath. "Things were happening much too quickly. Thank you, Forrest. Most men wouldn't be so gracious about calling a halt."

"Well, I do want to make love with you. You're a very desirable woman. You're also a beautiful, intelligent, and fascinating woman. Kissing you, Jillian, turned me inside out, and I knew I was losing control. You were responding to me, too, I could feel it."

"Yes," she said quietly, "I was."

"This may sound like a bunch of bull, some old-fashioned garbage, but the truth of the matter is," he went on, "I don't engage in casual sex. I never did, not even before the issue of safe sex came to public attention."

Jillian looked at him intently.

"When I'm with a woman, I have to care for her, about her. I've never been in love, but at least emotions of caring and respect have to be present. That takes it out of the sex arena and into the making-love arena. That means a lot to me, it really does."

He looked directly into her eyes.

"I don't know you well enough to have any idea as to your stand on sex, Jillian, but I'm very aware of mine. If, when, we make love, it will be exactly that—making love."

"Oh," she said softly. Then, for the life of her, she couldn't think of another thing to say.

She had never before, she realized, met a man like Forrest MacAllister, who had such old-fashioned values and self-imposed code of conduct. The men she'd dated in the past were ready, willing, and able to engage in casual sex on the first date.

She'd discussed it with Deedee once, and they'd agreed that the "no" had to come from the woman. But not so with Forrest. What an unusual and delightful man.

As for her response to Forrest's kiss—she'd returned it in total abandon—and the incredibly sensual sensations that had swept through her, she would discuss that with herself . . . later.

Several minutes passed in comfortable silence, each lost in their own thoughts.

"Forrest," Jillian said suddenly, "do you like boats?"

"Boats? Sure."

"Well, I have some friends who own a cabin cruiser that I'm welcome to borrow because they're on a trip to Greece. Would you like to go out in it tomorrow?"

"I was going to go look at a house with Michael that he's just contracted to restore, but—"

"That's work, you know. Wouldn't you like to have a carefree day?"

He nodded. "Yes, that sounds great. But what about you? Your strict schedule due to deadlines?"

"I'm on vacation," she said, smiling brightly.

"Good for you." Hallelujah and score one for the Angels and Elves. "You decided to take some time off, and you're doing it."

"Well, it's more complicated than that, but the bottom line is I'm on vacation."

"I'd love to go out on the water tomorrow, Jillian. We'll have to bundle up good because it'll be cold, but it sounds like fun."

"I'll pack a picnic lunch." She laughed. "Correct that. I've got a snazzy hamper someone gave me for Christmas a few years ago. We can stop at a deli on the way to the marina and fill it to the brim."

"What time shall I pick you up in the morning?"

"Make it ten o'clock. When I'm on vacation, I indulge myself in sleeping in late."

"I'll be here at ten o'clock on the dot." He glanced at his watch, then rolled to his feet in a smooth motion. "It's getting late. I'm going to head home and read another one of your novels. I borrowed all of them from Andrea."

Jillian got to her feet. "You did?"

"Yep," he said, pushing his feet into his shoes, "I did." He sat down on the edge of the sofa to tie his laces.

"I've heard that an author reveals something of herself in everything she writes."

"*I* don't."

He stood again, then crossed the room to pick up his jacket.

"Are you positive of that?" he said, looking at her.

"Of course. I'm the one writing the books, remember? They're drawn totally from my imagination."

"Maybe, maybe not."

"Well, I'm not going to debate the subject. I'll walk you to the door."

Forrest rolled down his cuffs, buttoned them, then shrugged into his jacket. At the front door, he encircled Jillian with his arms and kissed her deeply before she could speak further.

"Good night," he said, then released her. "I'll be here at ten in the morning."

Jillian nodded, not even attempting to answer. She was convinced that there was not one breath of air left in her body after that kiss.

Forrest opened the door and left the house, closing the door behind him with a quiet click. Jillian stood statue-still, allowing herself the luxury of reliving the kisses shared with Forrest—every sensual detail.

When heated desire began to pulse within her once again, she spun around and marched back into the living room. As she flopped down onto the sofa, she told herself that Forrest was no longer in the house and, therefore, she should automatically stop thinking about him.

Fat chance, she thought, mentally throwing up her hands in defeat. Forrest was not easily dismissed from a woman's mind. And her body? Good grief, it was going absolutely nuts.

"Perdition, Jillian," she said aloud. "What is your problem?"

Forget it, she decided in the next instant. She had postponed the internal discussion with herself regarding her startling responses to Forrest's kiss and touch. Now she was going beyond postponing. She was *canceling* the inner dialogue. Forrest was The Project, nothing more.

Yes, all right, she knew she had been swept away to an unknown place when Forrest had kissed her. But since she was fully aware of her unsettling reactions to him, she was in fine shape.

"You're splendidly in control, Ms. Jones-Jenkins," she said, with a decisive nod. "You may carry on with The Project."

She would read a book until she was sleepy enough to go to bed, she mused, getting to her feet. As per her vacation routine, it would be a novel far removed from the kind she wrote. She'd read a thriller, scare the socks off herself, and have a wonderful time.

What a satisfying feeling it was to know she was in complete charge of her own life.

Five

The next day was clear but crisp, typical weather for February.

Jillian dressed in jeans, tennis shoes, and a fisher-man's-knit sweater, then took a flannel-lined wind-breaker from the closet. She set the jacket next to the empty picnic hamper, along with a canvas tote bag that would serve as her purse for the outing. She'd called the marina manager earlier and arranged to have gas put in the boat. She was ready to go. *At nine o'clock,* she thought, rolling her eyes heavenward.

She always slept late during her vacation, the lazy mornings being one of her indulgences. But today? Her eyes had popped open at 7:00 a.m., and she'd known in-stantly that there was no chance of her drifting back into blissful sleep.

She glanced at her watch.

Nine-oh-two. This was ridiculous. At this rate, it would seem as though a week had passed before Forrest arrived. She'd write a newsy letter to her parents about the high points of the book-signing tour. Excellent idea.

The letter was written, sealed, stamped, and outside in the mailbox to be picked up by the postman by nine forty-five.

With a snort of self-disgust, she wandered around the living room, straightening throw pillows that didn't need straightening, picking up and setting back in place a variety of knickknacks, watering plants that had already been tended to by the housekeeper.

Oh, bother, she fumed, she was acting like an adolescent waiting for the captain of the high-school football team to pick her up for a date. What in the blue blazes was the matter with her? Her behavior was absurd.

At the sound of a car approaching, Jillian started quickly toward one of the front windows, then stopped dead in her tracks. She forced herself to sit down in an easy chair, and began to examine her fingernails as though they were the most fascinating ten little things she'd ever seen.

When Forrest rang the doorbell, she decided, she would count to sixty before she went to answer the summons. Very good.

Forrest got out of his car and stood quietly for a moment, his gaze sweeping over Jillian's house.

It really was attractive, he mused. It was similar to the one Andrea had designed for her and John, and was a popular style in that area of California. He liked it, and he liked the way Jillian had decorated the interior.

Jillian. He'd read another of her books after returning to his apartment the night before, and had thoroughly enjoyed it.

The hero had been the captain of a sailing ship. The heroine had managed to stow away on the vessel to escape marrying a lecherous older man her heartless father had promised her to.

After a rocky beginning to their relationship, they had slowly fallen in love and shared many adventures, including an escape from the evil clutches of the vengeful would-be husband.

In the end, the hero had given up his life on the high seas to settle down on land and run a shipping company. The happy couple had selected a house, set a date for the wedding, and were discussing how many children they wanted as the story drew to a close.

Ah, fantasy, Forrest thought wistfully. Jillian's novel had produced for the hero and heroine all the things *he* wanted for himself—love, a wife, children, a home.

But in the era Jillian had written about, the heroine didn't have a demanding career outside the home. In present times, what he wanted simply wasn't his to have. Two-career marriages did *not* meet his standards of how a family should function. Damn.

He pushed aside his bleak thoughts and headed for the front door, eager to begin the outing with Jillian. And eager to have her open the door so he could be the recipient of one of her sunshine smiles.

At the door, he pressed the bell, hearing it chime inside the house.

"Twenty-eight, twenty-nine," Jillian said, "and thirty."

She jumped to her feet.

A person just didn't realize how long sixty seconds were until she started counting them off. *Thirty* seconds were certainly enough of a delay.

She started toward the entry hall, ignoring the fact that she was practically running. When she flung the door open, the smile that lit up her face was genuine.

Forrest MacAllister, her mind hummed. And she was very, *very* glad to see him.

"Hi," she said, stepping back. "Come in." Sinful. Forrest in faded jeans, a dark blue sweater, and a white windbreaker was so ruggedly handsome it was sinful. "How are you this morning?" She closed the door behind him.

"I'm ready to sail the high seas," he said, matching her smile. How was it possible that each time he saw Jillian she appeared even more lovely? "I wish I had one of those shirts with the billowing sleeves like Roman wears."

"Roman?" Jillian repeated, obviously confused. "*My* Roman?"

"Yes, the hero in *Rapture in the Wind*. I read it last night. Great book, really great."

"Well, thank you, sir," she said, dipping her head slightly. "I'm glad you enjoyed it. We'd better be on our way. We have to stop at a deli and fill up the picnic hamper."

"Sure, let's go." He paused, no hint of a smile remaining. "I came in here talking a blue streak, and didn't greet you the way I intended."

"You didn't?"

He took one step to close the distance between them, then framed her face in his hands. A shiver coursed through Jillian as she looked directly into the warm brown depths of his eyes.

"No, Jillian, I didn't."

Forrest's mouth melted over hers, his tongue slipping between her parted lips.

Jillian placed her hands around his waist, then moved them up his back, savoring the feel of the taut muscles beneath her palms. She met his questing tongue with her own, the now familiar heat of desire beginning to pulse through her. He tasted like minty toothpaste, smelled like soap and fresh air, felt like heaven itself.

The kiss deepened and their hearts beat with wild tempos.

Forrest finally lifted his head and drew a ragged breath.

"Good morning, Jillian," he said, his voice gritty with passion.

"Good morning, Forrest," she whispered.

Slowly, reluctantly, they stepped back, dropping their hands to their sides, seeing their desire mirrored in the smoky hues of each other's eyes. The sensual mist that had encased them began to fade into oblivion. They were once again in Jillian's entry hall.

The kiss was over, but not forgotten.

"We're off, fair maiden," Forrest said, pointing one finger in the air. "Mayhap we shall encounter pirates on the seas, but fear not, for I shall protect you against the miscreants."

"Oh, good night," she said, with a burst of laughter. "Who writes your dialogue?"

"I do," he said, grinning. "Pretty good, huh?"

"Stick with architecture, Forrest. Or as we say in the business, 'Don't quit your day job.'"

"Oh."

Two hours later, they were surrounded by water as Forrest steered the twenty-five-foot cabin cruiser with expertise. Jillian sat on a stool next to where he stood, the semienclosed bridge sheltering her from the wind.

The ocean was choppy and appeared more green than blue. The sky that had been bright and clear earlier was now a blue gray, and dotted with darkening clouds.

"We'd better tune in to the Coast Guard weather channel," Forrest said. "We don't want to get caught out here in a storm."

Jillian tended to the radio, adjusting it by following instructions on a card taped to it.

"Even though it's a little choppy," Forrest said, "there's still a peacefulness about being on the water. There's no one else within our view, either."

"And no telephone, no computer," Jillian added, ticking off the items on her fingers. "No galleys, no deadline, no—"

"Got it," he said, laughing. "You're on vacation today."

She nodded decisively. "In spades."

"I respect that. If you put your mind to it, I bet you could have a very healthy balance of work and play in your life. A lot of people don't, you know. They get centered on their careers, and there isn't room for anything else. You've at least got an idea of how it *should* be."

That was debatable, Jillian mused. According to Deedee, Lorraine, some of her other friends, and even her agent, she was a workaholic during the months she was writing a book. Except for occasional outings, she only surfaced during the adventuresome two-week hiatuses that occurred two or three times a year.

Should she explain all that to Forrest? No, it wasn't necessary. For all she knew, he would be long gone before her two weeks were up, not completing his stint of being The Project. She might not even have enough time to shape up *his* attitudes toward balancing work and play.

Jillian glanced quickly at Forrest, then stared unseeing at the churning water.

A strange sense of emptiness had swept over her, she realized, as she'd entertained the prospect of Forrest walking out of her life.

Perdition, Jillian, she admonished herself. Stop being ridiculous. It didn't matter which one of them faded into the sunset first, because at the end of her vacation their time together would be over. Finished. Kaput. That funny feeling in her stomach had been...hunger. Yes, of course, that was it. She was hungry.

"Forrest, there's a cove a few miles up ahead. It might not be quite so windy there, the water calmer, and we could eat lunch without having to chase all the food across the table."

"Sounds good. Let's check it out."

The cove was edged with trees that acted as a windbreak and the water was smoother. Forrest cut the engine, dropped anchor, and they went below. The cabin was small, but every inch had been put to use. The decor was dark wood with kelly green accents.

The table where Jillian placed the containers of food she took from the hamper was bolted to the floor. The minuscule stove and refrigerator had always reminded her of dollhouse furniture, she told Forrest, and she adored the double bed, which was surrounded by built-in drawers on all four sides.

"It's like sleeping in a secret cave," she said, sitting down at the table.

Forrest chuckled as he sat opposite her. "That's your writer's imagination at work. Someone else would probably say the bed was a hole-in-the-wall where the carpenter got tired of making drawers."

"Architecture, Forrest," she said, laughing. "Stick to architecture."

All traces of his smile faded. "I really like your laughter. It's a delightful sound, like wind chimes or tinkling bells."

"I... Thank you. That was a lovely thing to say."

They continued to gaze at each other, losing track of time, feeling the embers of desire within them begin to grow hotter once again, threatening to burst into consuming flames.

"Hungry," Jillian said finally, her voice sounding strange to her own ears.

"Oh, yes," Forrest said, nodding.

She shook her head slightly. "For lunch. I'm hungry for *lunch*." She tore her gaze from Forrest's and reached for a plate. "We certainly bought a lot of different things. This is going to be a gourmet feast."

Forrest began to fill a plate while commanding himself to cool off, think about food, and *not* about grabbing Jillian up and carrying her to the "bed-in-the-wall" where the carpenter had run out of steam.

They ate without speaking for several minutes, while the boat rocked gently in the secluded cove.

"You know," Forrest said, slicing through the silence, "I've read two of your books so far. You've said that while some authors might reveal portions of themselves in their work, *you* don't. However, I did pick up on a common theme in both novels."

Jillian glanced up at him. "Oh?" She took a bite of crab salad.

"Trust. You put a lot of emphasis on trust. Not only did the heroines trust the heros to protect them from physical harm, but emotions were involved, as well. The heroes and heroines came to trust each other with their love, the essence of themselves. They rendered themselves vulnerable, laying it all on the line, and trusting each other to treat that love as the precious gift that it is. In both books there were conversations concerning the extreme importance of trust."

"Well, goodness," Jillian said, forcing a lightness into her voice, "I'd better be on the alert for the glaring error of repeating myself from one book to the next. That is a definite no-no. Although in this particular case..." Her voice trailed off.

"In this case?" he prompted.

"The importance of trust in a loving relationship could be justifiably addressed in every one of my books. Without trust, what do two people actually have? Nothing. It's the foundation that love is centered on, a solid base from which it can grow, if nurtured."

She leaned forward, her voice ringing with conviction when she continued speaking.

"If the trust isn't there, the couple is fooling themselves, mistaking lust for love. If it *is* present, then later destroyed, the relationship is over, beyond repair."

"That's a pretty hard stand on the issue."

Jillian moved back again, folding her arms over her breasts. "It's the way I feel, what I believe."

"Interesting, especially when you consider the fact that you claim that nothing of *you*, per se, is in any of your novels."

"Oh." She felt a warm flush on her cheeks. "Well, I..." She frowned.

"Don't stress, Jillian," he said, smiling. "I obviously want to get to know you better, or I wouldn't be here today. What's the harm in garnering some details through your books?'' He shrugged. ''Makes sense to me.''

''It certainly does not. How will you know what might be my opinions and views, and what are imaginary likes and dislikes I gave the characters to make them more believably human?''

''Well . . .''

''For example—'' she snatched up a breadstick and waggled it at Forrest ''—in the book that's in production at my publisher's now, the heroine has a good-luck charm. It's a little seashell that she always has with her. It might be in her pocket, her reticule, or in a small velvet pouch attached to a ribbon around her neck. She is never without it. When she gives it to the hero as he's about to go dashing off to face the villain, the hero realizes how deeply she loves him.''

''Your point?''

''My point is,'' she continued, her volume rising as she waved the breadstick in the air, ''I have never owned a good-luck charm in my life. You could, in the present state of your tiny mind, assume I personally have a thing for good-luck charms. You would be drawing a conclusion about me that would be totally wrong.''

Forrest snagged her wrist as it went whizzing by, and took a bite of the breadstick. As he chewed, he stared thoughtfully at the ceiling. After taking a sip of soda, he looked at Jillian again, seeing the very-pleased-with-herself expression on her face.

''Nope,'' he said, ''I wouldn't be wrong at all. Why? I'll be happy to explain.''

''Whoopee,'' she said dryly. ''I can hardly wait.''

''You're getting grumpy, Lady Jillian. Are you going to eat the rest of that breadstick?''

She smacked it into his hand.

"Thank you. To continue—I wouldn't focus on the good-luck charm itself, wouldn't go charging out to buy you a rabbit's foot to make a favorable impression on you. I would look *beyond* the charm."

"To what?"

"It's to *whom.* You. What message did you convey when the heroine gave the hero her special seashell? Trust. It's there again, Jillian, loud and clear."

Easy, MacAllister, he told himself. Don't push too hard. But, damn, he'd bet his last dime that Jillian's marriage had been shattered, and that she had been deeply hurt by a betrayal of trust by the man she'd chosen as her life's partner.

What *he* wanted was for her to trust *him* enough to tell him about what had happened. But she wasn't ready for that yet, not even close. Why was her trusting him to that degree so important? Hell, he had no idea.

"End of dissertation," he said lightly. "I'm going to have some of that strawberry cheesecake. It's calling my name. How about you?"

"What? Oh, no, I don't think so. Maybe I'll have some later."

Perdition *and* damn it, she thought. She felt terribly exposed, as though Forrest had physically pulled away her protective wall to peer into her heart, her mind, her very soul.

How had he managed to do that? She didn't know, but she didn't like it. Not one little bit.

And it was *not* going to happen again.

Six

As Jillian began to pack the empty containers back into the picnic hamper, she looked at Forrest in surprise when he immediately moved to help her.

His mother, Forrest explained cheerfully, had made it clear early on that there was no such thing in the Mac-Allister household as "women's work." They were a family, pure and simple, and everyone would pitch in no matter what the task entailed.

"Hooray for Mom," Jillian said, smiling.

"She's terrific," he said, nodding. "We all know how to cook, clean, sew on a button, sort and wash clothes, the whole nine yards. By the same token, Andrea can change a tire, check the oil in her car, fix a leaky faucet—you know, male stuff. It's a good program."

"Indeed it is," Jillian said, nodding. "That's the type of innovative ideas needed in two-career marriages, which you are so stubbornly convinced are a major disaster from the onset."

"They are. Look, so the guy helps clean the kitchen after dinner. Then what? He disappears into his den with a briefcase full of papers he's brought home. Or maybe it's the wife who has to work through the evening. Where's the quality family time? The kids get short-changed."

"It doesn't have to be that way, Forrest. Where is it written that a person has to bring work home night after night?"

Forrest placed a plastic container of a few remaining green grapes in the hamper, then straightened, looking directly at Jillian.

"In the corporate world you have to really scramble if you want to keep up with the competition. Don't you work into the evenings a great deal?"

"Well, yes, but..."

"I rest my case."

"Well, I'm not resting mine. I work evenings because I'm free to do so. I'm accountable only to myself. As a husband and father, you could decide that once you come home at night, your first priority would be your family."

"Not if I wanted to provide for them the way I see myself doing in my mind. Nope, it won't work, not in today's economy."

"Darn it, Forrest, you have a closed mind on the subject. You're putting too much emphasis on work, work, work. You've narrowed your existence down to slaving away over blueprints."

"That's how it has to be. *Your* main focus is your career, too."

"But I don't want the same things you do. You'd like a family. I'm perfectly content on my own."

"Are you?" he said quietly.

"Yes. Yes, I am. Absolutely. But you? Forrest, you've got to get your act together, your head on straight. You're going to sentence yourself to a lonely existence if you don't stop and consider some alternatives to the way you're thinking. Two-career marriages are flourishing all around you, but you're only paying attention to the ones that aren't. Are you listening to me?"

"At the volume that you're yelling, how could I *not* be listening?"

"I'm not yelling!" She paused, then sighed. "Yes, I am." She sank back onto her chair. "Ignore me."

Forrest leaned across the table and planted a quick kiss on her forehead.

"Impossible," he said. "I'd have to be dead to be able to ignore you while I'm with you. I can't ignore you when I'm *not* with you. I think about you a great deal when we're apart, Jillian."

She looked up at him. "I think about you, too, Forrest," she said, rather dreamily. In the next instant, her eyes widened and she stiffened. "I did *not* say that."

Forrest moved around the table to where Jillian sat and pulled her gently to her feet, wrapping his arms around her. She stared at his chest.

"Look at me," he said gently.

She raised her head slowly, her expression troubled when she met his gaze.

"Jillian, I don't quite understand why you're suddenly so flustered, stressed, upset, whatever it is you are. We were talking about genderless household chores, for Pete's sake."

"But we moved on to the subject of working too hard, how it affects a marriage, and on and on. I just hate knowing you won't ever be totally happy because you'll miss having a family."

"And you're dead set against ever having a family," he said. Jillian had tried marriage, it had failed. She'd been hurt, and he'd bet money that she wasn't about to go down that road again.

"Well, not everyone wants the same things from life, Forrest."

"True, that's true," he agreed, nodding.

But what, he wondered, was a man supposed to do when he met someone who was poles apart from him as far as what they wanted, but there was something new and special of incredible intensity and depth happening between them? He wanted to know what it was, what it meant.

Oh, man, this whole thing was crazy. He wanted to get married and have a family. Jillian didn't. He felt it was impossible for him to have said family because of the economy making it necessary for both parents to have careers. Jillian believed that dual-career marriages could function just fine with the proper compromises.

The wrong attitudes and beliefs were tacked onto the wrong people in this scenario. If he was smart, he'd cash in his chips and exit stage left before he went out of his beleaguered mind. But he'd never claimed to be a genius.

He did not want, nor did he intend, to walk out of Jillian Jones-Jenkins's life. He should, but he wouldn't, just couldn't.

Well, at least there was one thing they agreed on: trust. He knew how she felt about trust between a man and a woman, and her beliefs matched his own.

Forrest suddenly stiffened. "Thunder," he said, his head snapping up. "We'd better see what's happening with the weather. That's thunder rumbling in them there hills, ma'am."

He gave her a fast, hard kiss, released her, and headed for the stairs. Jillian was right behind him.

On the deck of the boat, they came to an abrupt halt as they saw the heavy dark clouds covering the sky, and the trees lining the cove whipped into a frenzy by a rapidly rising wind.

"Holy smoke," Forrest said.

"We'd better get on the radio," Jillian said. "It's ship-to-shore, and we can contact the Coast Guard and ask what we should do."

They ran to the bridge as lightning zigzagged across the sky and thunder continued to rumble in a nearly steady cadence.

Forrest quickly read the instructions on the laminated card taped to the radio, and minutes later was communicating with the man on duty at the Coast Guard station. As they talked, big drops of cold rain began to fall, being flung in all directions by the wind.

"Roger," Forrest finally said. "Thank you, and over and out." He grabbed Jillian's hand. "Let's get below," he yelled, above the roar of the wind.

Even though the distance from the bridge to the stairway was short, they were thoroughly soaked by the time they got below deck. The boat rocked back and forth, and the picnic hamper began to slide across the table.

"Whoa," Forrest said, snatching up the hamper and setting it on the floor.

Jillian wrapped her hands around her elbows, unable to stop her teeth from chattering. "Oh-h-h, I'm freezing, turning into an icicle."

"You heard the radio transmission," Forrest said. "The Coast Guard wants us to stay put until this blows over. They said we're safer in this cove than on the open water. We've got to get out of these wet clothes before we catch pneumonia. Do you know what the setup is here for light, heat, hot water?"

Jillian nodded, tightening her hold on her arms. "There's an independent generator that services lights, that space heater on the wall, and a small hot-water tank. I doubt that there are any spare clothes on board other than extra bathing suits, but there's a stack of beach towels in the center drawer beneath the bed."

"Okay. Good."

Forrest turned on two lamps mounted on the wall, which cast a soft glow over the area. Opening the drawer Jillian had indicated, he removed four large, brightly colored towels. He crossed the room and gave two of them to her.

"You go ahead and shower," he said. "I'll do a quick inspection to see if there's anything that needs securing. We're in for a bumpy ride, or float, or whatever."

Jillian nodded and hurried to enter the small enclosure she referred to as a bathroom, knowing that nautical jargon said it was the head, which she'd always thought was rather silly.

With difficulty, she managed to peel off her wet jeans, then the remainder of her clothing. She sighed with relief when she stepped into the shower stall and felt the welcome spray of warm water cascading over her chilled body.

She'd have to hurry, she knew, as there was not a great deal of hot water provided by the minisize tank.

Minutes later she stepped out of the stall, and vigorously rubbed her hair with the huge, thirsty towel. She dried the rest of herself until her skin was pink.

Now what? she thought suddenly. Her clothes were soaking wet, including her bra and panties. The towel she'd already used was damp, so— Good grief, she had nothing to wear except the second beach towel. Well, so be it. The only other choice was to walk out of there naked as the day she was born.

She finger-combed her hair into a semblance of order, wrapped the towel around herself like a sarong that fell to just above her knees, and tucked the flap of the towel between her breasts. Picking up her wet clothes and the damp towel, she took a deep, steadying breath, plastered a smile on her face, and opened the door.

"It's all yours," she said breezily. Her gaze swept over the room, taking in the beach towels spread on the table and over the backs of the chairs.

"We can put our clothes on these," Forrest said, placing a towel on the last chair. "Hopefully they'll dry out a bit, and the furniture won't be damaged. I turned on the heat and—" He looked up at Jillian and stopped speaking. "Holy smoke," he whispered.

Jillian walked forward and dumped her clothes in the center of the table.

Do *not*, she told herself, look at that man. She'd heard his hoarsely whispered reaction to her apparel, or lack of same. She was acutely aware of the fact that she was naked beneath that towel, and Forrest was not a stupid person. She didn't want to see what message might be radiating from his expression, or from the depths of those incredible brown eyes of his.

She busied herself with her clothes, letting out a whoosh of breath as she heard the water in the shower.

Hesitating when she picked up her soggy lace bra and panties, she mentally shrugged, deciding that a virile man like Forrest MacAllister had no doubt seen his share of woman's undies.

Her laundry tended to, she glanced around for a place to sit. There was a small, cushioned seat against one wall that was the top of a storage box. She'd sat on it in the past, and it was as hard as a rock.

No contest. She was declaring first-come-first-served, and claiming the bed. Forrest could plunk himself on the bench.

She took one of the pillows from beneath the spread and placed it against the back wall. Crawling over the bed, she sat straight up, legs extended, facing the room. After checking to be certain her towel was secure, she folded her hands primly in her lap.

In the next moment, she decided she looked like a Victorian maiden on her wedding night. She crossed her ankles, striving for a more nonchalant pose, then stared at her hands, wondering what on earth to do with them.

"A magazine," she said. "Yes. Perfect."

Hearing the water stop running in the shower, she scrambled off the bed, nearly losing the towel in the process, dashed across the room to snatch a magazine out of a holder mounted on the wall, then hightailed it back to the bed.

The towel was straightened, her ankles crossed in a casual mode, and her nose was buried in the magazine she held up in front of her face, when Forrest returned to the main room.

"That shower was heaven itself," he said. "Man, that felt good."

"Mmm," Jillian said, not looking at him.

"These clothes are sure wet, considering we weren't out in the rain that long."

"Mmm."

"The boat isn't rocking too badly. We'll pretend it's a giant-size cradle."

"Mmm."

Forrest crossed the room and wiggled one of Jillian's big toes. "Hey, you."

She gasped in shock, and smacked the magazine onto her lap.

And then she stopped breathing as she stared up at Forrest MacAllister.

He was beautiful, she mused, finally taking a breath. He'd tucked the towel around his waist, allowing it to fall to midcalf. The soft light made his tanned skin appear like polished bronze. The broad, bare expanse of his chest caused her fingers to itch with the urge to tangle in the mass of damp auburn curls, then slide over the taut, perfectly proportioned muscles of his arms.

Masculinity personified, her mind hummed. Gorgeous. Blatantly male. And naked as a jaybird beneath a scrap of terry cloth.

"Jillian?"

"Who?" she said, then blinked. "I mean . . . what?"

Forrest picked up the other pillow. "Move over."

"Why?"

"Because we're going to be here for a while, toots, and I'm not sitting on that brick of a bench. There are wet clothes on all the chairs, so . . . please move over and share the bed."

Share the bed, her mind echoed. They were going to share the bed. This bed, the one she was sitting on in the secret cave created by the lazy carpenter, was the one they were going to share.

Jillian, stop it, she ordered herself. She was getting hysterical. She could handle this. She was a mature woman, not a flaky adolescent. *Yes! She was woman!* But, oh, dear heaven, Forrest was the epitome of man.

"Hey!" he said.

"Yes, I'm sharing. I'm moving over right now. Here I go, wiggling right over here." She clutched the towel at the center of her breasts, then readjusted the pillow. "There. Now you have room. Go for it, MacAllister." She grabbed the magazine and placed it in front of her face again, close to her nose.

She was tense from head to toe as she felt Forrest move onto the bed, prop his pillow next to hers, squirm around, then settle into place.

A long, silent minute ticked by.

"Interesting," Forrest said finally.

"Hmm?" she said, her undivided attention directed toward the magazine.

"You have many facets, Lady Jillian. I wouldn't have thought you'd be so engrossed in a *Popular Mechanics* magazine."

Jillian's eyes widened as she comprehended for the first time what she was holding.

"Well, of course, I'm interested," she said, turning a page. "One never knows when one might need to do something mechanical . . . and popular."

"Oh," he said, with a burst of laughter.

"It's true," she said firmly. "I own a home, you know. Things need fixing at times."

"*Popular* things," he said, still smiling.

"Whatever," she mumbled.

"Tell me something, Jillian."

"Hmm?" She turned another page.

"How can you see to read? Those lights I turned on are pretty dim. It's very shadowy back here in your secret cave. You must have remarkable vision."

Jillian squinted at the magazine. "Oh." She snapped her head around to look at him, and nodded. "I do. Oh my, yes, I have excellent vision. Superb vision, as a matter of fact. I— Aaak!" she yelled, in the next instant.

The boat had suddenly seemed to lift nearly out of the water, then tilt to one side. The magazine flew in one direction, Jillian in the other—toward Forrest.

As she sprawled across his lap, his arms shot out, one wrapping around her beneath her breasts, the other under her knees. He scooped her up and planted her firmly on his lap. The boat returned to the gently rocking motion.

"Easy does it, there," Forrest said. "Either some idiot was whizzing past at the end of the cove, or the Coast Guard went by, but we're all right now. Everything is under control."

Except Jillian Jones-Jenkins, she thought frantically. She was perched on Forrest MacAllister's lap, for crying out loud. Her heart was doing the tango, and the heat... Oh, dear heaven, the heat within her was churning and pulsing, low and deep. Everything was under control? That was the most ridiculous thing she'd ever heard.

"Jillian," Forrest said, his voice quiet as he looked directly into her eyes.

And she was lost.

No longer could she resist the urge to sink her fingers into the auburn curls on the muscled wall of Forrest's chest.

And so, she did.

No longer could she keep from inhaling, then savoring, his scent of soap and man.

And so, she did.

No longer could she ignore the fact that only two terry-cloth towels separated her from him, making her acutely aware of the rock-hard feel of his thighs beneath the softness of her own. She wanted to rejoice in the magnificence of his masculinity compared to her own femininity.

And so, she did.

No longer could she ignore the raspy sound of Forrest's quickened breathing as he continued to gaze into her eyes, nor the tempting sight of his lips so very close to hers. She wanted to kiss those lips, taste them again, meet his tongue with her own.

And so... she did.

She slipped one hand to the back of his head, burying her fingers in his thick hair, and spread her other hand flat on his chest, feeling the rapid beat of his heart. She leaned forward and claimed his lips.

A groan rumbled in Forrest's throat as he met her mouth eagerly, urgently. He moved his arm from under her knees to wrap it around her, his other arm still firmly beneath her breasts.

His arousal was instantaneous. Heavy, aching, pressing against Jillian with the declaration of his want, his burning need. He jerked his head to break the kiss.

"Jillian," he said, then drew a rough breath. "I want to make love with you. *Make love, Jillian.* You can be certain of that. What's happening here is important, very special." Something that was becoming much, much more than an Angels and Elves assignment.

"Yes," she whispered. "Yes, Forrest, I want to make love with you, too."

Jillian? her mind nudged. What are you doing? *Think.* Forrest is The Project. He'll be gone in less than two weeks. *Jillian!*

But she ignored the niggling little voice, pushed aside the warnings of her mind, and listened only to her heart.

Yes, yes, yes, she wanted to make love with Forrest.

"Yes," she whispered again.

He captured her mouth once more in a searing kiss, and she leaned into it, taking all he gave, giving in return with total abandon. He pulled the end of her towel free, allowing the material to drop into a colorful pool at her hips. He cupped one breast in his hand, stroking the nipple to a taut bud with his thumb. Jillian whimpered with building passion.

Forrest ended the kiss and lifted her from his lap as though she weighed little more than a feather. He leaned forward and laid her on the bed, stretching out beside her in the next moment, resting on one forearm.

His eyes swept over her bare breasts; then, with a visibly shaking hand, he swept back the towel, revealing the rest of her body to his smoldering gaze. He flicked aside his own towel, exposing his arousal.

Their eyes explored eagerly, visually tracing every inch of each other, fanning the flames of desire burning within them.

"Beautiful," Forrest said. "You're so beautiful, Jillian."

"You're magnificent, you truly are."

He looked deep into her eyes, as though searching for, then finding, the answer to an unspoken question. He dipped his head to draw the soft flesh of one of her breasts deep into his mouth, his tongue laving the nipple in a steady rhythm.

Jillian closed her eyes for a moment to savor the exquisite sensations swirling within her.

Forrest moved to her other breast, paying homage to its sweet bounty. His hand skimmed over the flat plane of her stomach, then lower, and lower still, to the apex of her thighs.

She trembled from the tantalizing foray, one hand gripping the bunching muscles of his biceps.

Then Forrest's lips traveled the path his hand had taken. Jillian could feel the tension building within her, tightening into a heated coil that pulsed in the dark, moist center of her femininity. She tossed her head restlessly, a near sob escaping from her lips.

"Forrest, please," she whispered. "Please."

"Soon, Jillian," he said, hardly recognizing the sound of his own voice. "Soon."

Control, MacAllister, his mind hammered. He was slipping too close to the edge, wanted to seek release in the beckoning haven of Jillian's body—now. *Now.* But he had to regain a modicum of command over himself, because Jillian's pleasure must be assured. That concern was uppermost in his mind, with a fierce intensity he'd never experienced before.

"Forrest," Jillian said, her voice quivering.

He moved over her, resting his weight on both forearms, seeing the smoky-gray hue of desire radiating from Jillian's eyes. Her cheeks were flushed, her lips moist from his kisses, and parted slightly in an enticing invitation.

He kissed her, then raised his head again, wanting, needing, to see her face in the soft glow of the lights as they became one entity.

Slowly, so slowly, he entered her, a moan rumbling from his throat as he sheathed himself in the dark, moist heat.

Ecstasy.

Jillian sighed with pure feminine pleasure, savoring the sensation of Forrest meshing with her, the strength and power of what he was bringing to her. She could feel his muscles trembling from forced restraint where her hands splayed on his glistening back.

Her heart sang with joy at the realization that he was putting her pleasure before his own, telling her by his actions that they were indeed *making love,* that this *was* special.

But *his* pleasure was important to her as well, and she lifted her hips to draw him fully into her.

"Jillian..."

"I want you so much."

He began to move, increasing the cadence with each thrust, and she met him beat for urgent beat. The tension built within them to a sweet pain, taking them closer and closer to what they sought.

Then waves of passion swept through Jillian, seeming to carry her up and away, flinging her far beyond reason and reality to a glorious place.

"Forrest!"

Seconds later he joined her there, shuddering, with a sound that was thoroughly male, bursting from his throat. Spasm after spasm consumed them as though the ecstasy would last for all time.

They hovered in the beyond, then drifted back, Forrest collapsing against her, his last ounce of energy spent. He rolled onto his side, taking her with him.

Their breathing slowed. Their bodies cooled. Their heartbeats quieted to normal tempos. Their minds and hearts held the memories of what had just transpired, and they treasured them.

The boat continued to rock slowly back and forth, and the rain fell steadily, creating a symphony produced by nature.

Forrest drew the edges of the bedspread over them, then settled again, holding Jillian close, his lips resting lightly on her forehead.

Neither spoke as they lay in sated contentment, listening to the music of the rain.

Somnolence crept over them, and they slept.

Several hours later, Jillian stirred and opened her eyes, having no idea in her foggy state as to where she was. She turned her head, and her breath caught as she saw Forrest sleeping peacefully only inches away.

A soft smile touched her lips as she gazed at him. His strength emanated from his body even while he slept, yet there was a vulnerability there, too; an aura of trust that she found endearing.

Forrest MacAllister, her mind hummed.

She frowned as she tore her gaze from him to stare up at the bottom of the drawers built above the bed.

Sleep on, Forrest, she mentally directed him. Before he awakened, she needed time to sort and sift, to think about what had taken place between them.

She had made love with Forrest MacAllister.

There it was—a fact, right out in front of her—and it needed to be addressed.

Was she sorry? Did she regret her actions? Was she furious with herself for allowing her passion to override reason?

Narrowing her eyes, she focused inward, getting in touch with herself to find the answers to the questions.

And the answers were there, clear and precise—no, no, and no.

That's just dandy, Jillian Jones-Jenkins, she thought dryly. She knew where she stood on the issue, but what she didn't know was *why* she felt as she did. She should be calling herself a featherhead, a flibbertigibbet, a ninnyhammer, a . . . a dope.

She *knew* her time with Forrest was measured in days. There was no room in her life for a man or a relationship when she was writing a novel.

She'd had it all figured out as far as Forrest being The Project, but had now totally complicated things. Emotions had come into play when she'd made love with Forrest. They'd *made love*, not had casual sex, and from that realization came the confusion and muddled mess.

So, why didn't she regret what she had done?

Oh, fiddle, she didn't know.

Forrest would awaken soon, and she'd better have her head on straight. As any man would, under the circumstances, he'd be watching for what her mood, her attitude was, regarding what had transpired.

Well, so be it. She had *no* regrets, was *not* sorry. That was the truth, and was what Forrest deserved to know. That she was confused was *her* problem to deal with.

Having concluded the conversation between herself and herself, Jillian switched her attention to what was going on around her.

It was quite dark in the room, the small lamps on the wall casting circles of light over a few feet, and leaving the remainder of the expanse in deep shadow. The boat was still, and she realized there was no longer any sound of the musical rain.

Peering through the semidarkness, she squinted at the battery-operated clock on the wall, her eyes widening as she saw it was nearly six o'clock. She and Forrest had slept the afternoon away, blissfully sated.

"Forrest," she said, poking his chest with one finger. "Forrest, wake up."

"Mmm. Later," he mumbled.

Jillian laughed softly. Forrest muttered a few more words that she couldn't understand, then finally opened his eyes.

"Hi," she said.

He shook his head slightly, then a slow smile crept onto his lips.

"I was dreaming," he said, his voice husky with sleep.

The sexy sound caused a shiver to course through Jillian.

"I was Roman on my sailing ship, out on the high seas," Forrest went on. "I even had a terrific shirt with billowing sleeves. It was permanent-press, of course, because I really hate ironing."

"How nice," she said, matching his smile. "However, that was then and this is now, and it's six o'clock."

"You're kidding." He sat up. "No, you're not kidding." He paused. "The storm has passed through, I guess. I suppose we'd better head for the marina."

"Yes."

He shifted around to rest on one forearm as he looked directly into her eyes. No trace of a smile remained on his face.

"Jillian," he said quietly, "making love with you was incredibly beautiful and very special. I want you to know that."

"I feel the same way."

"No regrets?"

She hesitated for only a moment. "No, Forrest. No regrets."

He lowered his head and kissed her deeply. The embers of the passion still within them burst instantly into flames. When he lifted his head again, he drew a ragged breath.

"Nay, I say, MacAllister," he said, "or the very night shall pass on this vessel." He smiled. "That means, toots, that I've got to quit kissing you right now, or we'll be sharing a half-dozen green grapes for breakfast."

Jillian laughed, the enchanting sound causing the heated desire within Forrest to coil tighter.

She slid off the bed and crossed the room to where their clothes were spread over the table and chairs.

Forrest drank in the sight of her naked body, slender and soft, totally feminine, a perfect counterpart to the hard contours of his own. What he couldn't see in the shadows, his mind vividly supplied.

Lovely, he mused. Jillian was so beautiful. The lovemaking they'd shared had been exquisite. Not only had their bodies meshed, but there had been undefinable emotions entwined, as well.

It had been complex and rare, very different from anything he'd experienced before. There was, indeed, something important happening between them, and nothing would keep him from discovering what it was.

"The clothes are dry," Jillian said, bringing Forrest from his thoughts, "but stiff as a board." She began to dress. "I'm fantasizing about a warm bubble bath and a soft, cozy robe."

Forrest joined her at the table, reaching for his sweater. "I'm fantasizing about two or three hamburgers, a thick milk shake, and a double order of fries."

"Sold. Hamburgers, *then* a bubble bath."

"Your wish is my command. We'll share a meal, then share—"

"Wrong. You'll go home. *I'll* have a bubble bath."

"Perdition!"

Jillian dissolved in laughter and Forrest, infected by the wind-chime sound, laughed with her.

They were hungry, wearing wrinkled, scratchy clothes, and miles from shore and the comforts they yearned for, but their smiles remained firmly in place all the way back to the marina.

"Deedee?" Andrea said. "I hope I'm not calling during your dinner. Guess what? I haven't been able to reach Forrest or Jillian all day. I got their answering machines every time I phoned.

"I realize I shouldn't get carried away with that information, but at least there's a *chance* they might be together. If they are, I wonder how they got along for that many hours.

"Oh, wouldn't it be grim if they spent the day arguing?"

Seven

The next two days, and nights, flew by in a blur of activity. Jillian felt delightfully alive, invigorated, and was engaged in the best vacation she'd ever had.

On Friday she cleaned her closets, discarding clothes she no longer wanted, and making a list of what she needed to buy.

That night, she and Forrest attended a concert featuring a popular country-and-western singer. They both wore jeans, boots, and Western shirts with pearl snaps.

"My goodness," Jillian said, as they stood in her living room, "we look so authentic. We're awesome, Forrest, totally awesome."

Forrest hooked his thumbs in the front pockets of his jeans.

"Ma'am," he said, in a lazy Western drawl, "you ain't seen nothin' yet. Y'all come on outside with me, little lady."

To Jillian's laughing delight, Forrest had borrowed his brother Ryan's Jeep for the evening.

"*Now* we're authentic, ma'am," Forrest said.

"Drive this thing, cowboy. It's time to do the boot-scootin' boogie."

After the show, which they thoroughly enjoyed, they went to a Chinese restaurant. Unable to resist the tempting selections, they ordered enough food for four people.

"This is delicious," Jillian said, then took a bite of something with a name she couldn't pronounce.

"Yes, ma'am, it surely is," Forrest said.

Jillian laughed. "Forrest, your Western twang just isn't making it in a Chinese restaurant."

"Oh. Good point."

"You know," she said, thoughtfully, "this evening's outing is a perfect example of the kind of perks, per se, that a couple could have if they both worked."

"That's true. Concert tickets, then dinner out afterward, would take a big bite out of a married couple's single-income household budget. But where are the kids?"

"They're at home with a reliable, trustworthy sitter. We, the parents, need some hours alone together."

"How much time did we spend with our children during the week? We worked in the evenings. Right? We both have careers and we enjoy expensive entertainment like this evening's. Sunday we're taking the kids out to lunch, then to the zoo. That's a family outing. It also costs big bucks. One, or both of us, worked through the evenings."

"No, we did not," Jillian said, leaning toward him. "We compromised. There's that word that makes you break out in hives. *Compromise.* We went to the concert, then on home where we made ice-cream sundaes in our own kitchen."

"I see," he said, nodding slowly.

"Do you? On Sunday we'll pack a picnic lunch, then go to the zoo. Compromise, Forrest. Two careers, no slaving away with work every night at home, and nice outings as a couple, and others with the kids. If you weren't so stubbornly narrow-minded, you would realize you can have the wife and family you want, without anyone getting the short end of the stick."

"Well, you've certainly given me food for thought," he said, staring into space. "Michael's wife, Jenny, stays home with their son, Bobby, but now that I think about it, Michael and Jenny go out alone most weekends."

"Excellent. That's a one-income family compromising. There's no reason why people in a two-career marriage can't do the same thing."

"How many kids do we have?"

"What?" she said, frowning.

"How many little munchkins are we taking to the zoo on Sunday?"

"Have an egg roll, Forrest. You need fuel for your brain."

"Well, you made our family sound real," he said, smiling.

Jillian shrugged. "I'm a writer with a vivid imagination."

Forrest's smile faded. "And you, of course, don't want any part of the scenario you just painted so clearly."

Jillian met his gaze directly. "No. No, I don't."

"So, while I'm getting the hang of this compromise jazz, leaving my briefcase at the office, you're still working evenings."

"Because I can," she said, splaying one hand on her chest. "I don't have the family you do, who needs my attention."

"Jillian, did it ever occur to you that this famous compromise of yours should apply to you, too?"

"Whatever for?"

"For you. Don't you want more in your life besides work, with an occasional outing like the one we're sharing tonight?"

She lifted her chin. "My life is perfectly fine just the way it is, thank you very much."

"That's *your* opinion," he said, glaring at her.

Jillian opened her mouth to retort, then closed it, and shook her head.

"No, I'm not going any further with this discussion," she said, "because we're headed for an argument. Our evening together has been so lovely. Let's not spoil it, Forrest." She smiled. "Have that egg roll."

He picked up one of the treats, matching her smile. "Sold. I *do* intend to think about what you said, though. I've never had the compromise angle so clearly defined before. It has merit. Yep, food—" he took a bite of the egg roll "—for thought."

"Good," she said.

She was making marvelous progress with The Project, she mused. Yes sirree, she was scoring points in her Angels and Elves mission. It was just that... Well, a funny, cold knot had tightened in her stomach as she'd envisioned Forrest with a faceless wife and children. Oh, how ridiculous. *She* needed an egg roll.

"So," she said, "Michael and Jenny have a son. Right?"

"Oh, yeah, Bobby is one cute kid. Did I tell you that I won The Baby Bet when he was born?"

"The what?"

"It was a high-tech bet. There were too many of us involved in it to go for a straight 'Is it a girl or boy?' So we added date of birth and—get this—time of day."

"*Very* high-tech."

"Indeed, and *I* won. I had the right sex, the right day, *and* I hit the time within twenty minutes. You're looking at The Baby Bet pro, here."

Jillian laughed in delight. "Your talents never fail to amaze me, Mr. MacAllister."

"Darlin'," he said, his voice low and rumbly, "to quote myself, you ain't seen nothin' yet."

Sudden and sensual pictures flitted into Jillian's mind of the lovemaking she'd shared with Forrest, and a warm flush crept onto her cheeks. She cleared her throat, then glanced over the table.

"It's fortune-cookie time," she said. "I can read it, but I can't eat it. I'll explode if I take one more bite." She broke open the crisp cookie and unfolded the narrow strip of paper, reading it quickly. "Oh."

"Oh?" Forrest leaned toward her. "That's a weird fortune. Let me see that." He took the paper from her hand, read it, then looked at her with a serious expression. "'You are about to experience a major change in your life on an emotional, not material plane.'"

The warm flush on Jillian's cheeks intensified, and was accompanied by heat that swirled through her. Desire was radiating from Forrest's dark brown eyes and was, she knew, mirrored in her own.

"Major emotional change," he repeated, a husky quality in his voice.

Jillian tore her gaze from his, aware that her hand was trembling slightly as she reached for the other cookie.

"Read *your* fortune now, Forrest," she said, handing it to him.

He crushed the cookie and pulled the paper free, hooting with laughter as he read the message.

Jillian peered over at the paper and smiled as she read it aloud: " 'Your ship cannot come in because it sank.' "

"Wrong," Forrest said. "They don't know who they're dealing with, here. Roman and I would never let our ships sink."

"Of course not," she said. "You'd get your snazzy shirts wet."

"You've got *that* straight."

"You're crazy."

"You're beautiful," he said, then gave her a quick, but toe-curling kiss. "Let's go home, Lady Jillian."

They made exquisite love far into the night in Jillian's bed. She was sleepily aware of Forrest leaving at dawn to go to his apartment to change clothes, and then on to play golf with Michael.

During the day on Saturday, Jillian talked to Deedee on the telephone to arrange lunch the next day, then a shopping spree. Deedee immediately agreed, stating she'd have Books and Books covered the entire afternoon by one of her part-time employees.

"So, what's new?" Deedee said.

"We'll get caught up at lunch."

"Promise? Cross your heart?"

"Well, sure, Deedee. We always chatter like magpies when we get together."

"I'll be counting the hours, Jillian."

"You're acting like a weird biscuit, Mrs. Hamilton. I'll see you tomorrow. Bye."

Deedee replaced the receiver on the telephone.

"A weird biscuit?" she said, to no one. "No-o-o, I'm a stressed-out Cupid."

The remainder of the day, Jillian ran errands. She went to the cleaners, the drugstore, ordered more business cards, and made the other stops on her list.

She hated errands, and usually assigned most of them to her secretary, Lorraine, but found herself in a chipper mood during the entire excursion.

So, okay, she mused, as she finally relaxed in a bubble bath, she had thought more about the evening ahead with Forrest as she'd dashed here and there, than about what she was actually doing at the time.

But that was understandable, she reasoned. Forrest was a handsome, charming, fun-to-be-with man. It made perfect sense that she was looking forward to dinner and dancing with Mr. MacAllister. It didn't constitute a "major emotional change," for heaven's sake.

And the lovemaking they'd shared? It was beautiful beyond description. The unnamed emotions that rose to the fore each time she was with Forrest were coming from a new and different place inside her.

Should she be attempting to define those emotions? she wondered, absently watching the bubbles pop in fragrant bursts. No, that wasn't necessary. Those emotions were intertwined with the lovemaking itself, were a part of the exquisite intimate act. It should all be wrapped up like a precious gift, a treasure to be cherished, then tucked away in her heart when Forrest was gone.

When Forrest was gone.

Jillian frowned as the words echoed in her mind. She stepped from the tub and began to dry herself with a fluffy, salmon-colored towel.

When Forrest was gone.

Now, Jillian, she admonished herself, shape up. She knew the facts as they stood, knew the level of self-discipline she had to maintain to achieve her career goals. Nothing was allowed to draw her away from her purpose when she was working. Nothing, and no one.

So, when her vacation was over, Forrest MacAllister would be gone.

Besides, she mentally rambled on, as she began to dress, she wanted no part of a serious relationship. Never again would she hand over her heart to another person, render herself totally vulnerable, she'd never again be defenseless and helpless as that heart was smashed to smithereens. She'd learned that lesson the hard and hurtful way, and would not make the same mistake again.

Fine, she thought, lifting her chin. At the end of her two-week hiatus, Forrest would be gone. So be it. The bright side of the picture was that she was making marvelous progress with her Angels and Elves mission. That was great. Right? Right.

During the evening, Jillian felt like Cinderella at the ball. The leisurely dinner was delicious, then they moved into a ballroom where a ten-piece band played dreamy music. Forrest was an excellent dancer, and when he took her into his arms, Jillian welcomed the wondrous sensations that consumed her.

She felt safe, protected, fragile and feminine. There was no reason to think; she needed only to feel, savor, allow the desire within her to build to a fever pitch.

Unlike Cinderella, she would not have to dash away at midnight. The entire night ahead was hers, to share with Forrest.

Although Jillian would have thought it impossible, their lovemaking that night was even more magical, more intense than before. She was unable at times to decipher their bodies as two separate entities. They were meshed, completely one, as they soared to their glorious place.

A few minutes after noon on Sunday, Jillian slid onto the chair opposite Deedee in a busy restaurant.

"Good, I'm only a couple of minutes late," Jillian said, smiling. "The traffic is grim."

"It's so good to see you, Jillian," Deedee said, matching her smile. "Let's order. I'm famished."

Jillian glanced at the menu, decided she would have a chef's salad, then observed Deedee while the other woman was engrossed in the list of selections.

Deedee was so pretty, Jillian mused. She was thirty-one, but appeared younger due to her delicate features, and she wore very little makeup. There was a fresh, wholesome aura about her, accentuated by a dusting of freckles across her nose.

No one would know that the perky, smile-always-at-the-ready woman had been tragically widowed eight years before when her husband had been killed flying an air-force jet in a training exercise.

After a year of intense grieving during which Deedee had barely functioned, she'd taken herself in hand, sought counseling, then used her husband's insurance money to create Books and Books.

Jillian had met her five years ago when Lorraine had arranged a book-signing session at the store. Their friendship had grown steadily, and little by little, Deedee had revealed the sad circumstances of her past.

Strange, Jillian thought, taking a sip of water. She had never told Deedee the details of her own marriage and

subsequent divorce. She'd simply said, as she had to
Forrest, that the marriage had been a terrible mistake and
was old news that wasn't worth discussing. Had it hurt
Deedee's feelings over the years to realize that Jillian
wasn't sharing her innermost secrets?

A waitress appeared, bringing welcome relief from
Jillian's suddenly troubled thoughts.

They ordered, then Deedee propped her elbows on the
table and folded her hands beneath her chin. Her short
hair was a mass of silky, strawberry-blond curls, and her
large brown eyes were sparkling with excitement.

Jillian laughed. "Okay, Mrs. Hamilton, tell all. You're
about to wiggle right out of that chair."

"I took the plunge."

"You're getting married?" Jillian asked, all inno-
cence.

Deedee wrinkled her freckle-dotted nose. "Good grief,
no, I am *not* getting married, Ms. Jones-Jenkins, and you
know it."

Jillian shrugged. "Just thought I'd ask. Tell me about
your plunge."

"Well, you know how intrigued I am by rare books.
I've collected more than two dozen over the years. It's
not a lot, but enough to plunge.

"So, even as we speak, a craftsman is making me a
special cupboard to hang on the wall behind the counter
at the store. It will have wire-threaded glass, and will be
kept locked. I'm going to start an advertising campaign
to let it be known that Books and Books now buys and
sells rare editions. I'm very excited."

"As well you should be. Oh, Deedee, that's marvelous. I know that dealing in rare books has been a dream
of yours. Okay, this lunch is on me to celebrate the ex-
panded service of Books and Books."

"Hear, hear. Speaking of the store, your novels have been selling like hotcakes ever since the book-signing session. You've been so supportive over the years with your willingness to do an autograph party for each of your books as they came out.

"That, plus all the author friends you begged and-or threatened to get to do autographings, enabled me to launch my rare-book dream much sooner than I'd hoped."

"It was my pleasure," Jillian said. "All my writer friends were very impressed with your store, by the way. They'd all be happy to come again."

"Thank you so much, Jillian."

The waitress arrived at that moment with their meals, and they ate in silence for several minutes.

"I've talked enough about me," Deedee finally said. "What have you been up to?"

"Oh," Jillian said, breezily, "a little of this, a little of that."

"Would you stop it?" Deedee said. "You're perfectly aware that I want to know if you made Forrest Mac-Allister The Project. You said you'd think about it, then went to the door to get a pizza."

"Well, the pizza turned out to be Forrest."

"What?"

Jillian explained how she'd made the dinner date with Forrest, but had been so exhausted she'd forgotten she'd done it. And, yes, yes, yes, nosy Deedee, Forrest was The Project. The man needed an attitude adjustment, and she was making great progress on the subject of his working far too much.

"That brings you up to date," Jillian said.

"Not quite. What about you? You're the other half of the dates between you and Forrest. Do you like him?"

"Yes."

Deedee stared at her for a long moment.

"That's it?" she said finally. "Yes? Come on, Jillian, could I have some details, here?"

"No."

Deedee's eyes widened. "Oh, my gosh, you and Forrest are lovers."

"Did I say that? I certainly did not."

"Your crisp little answers speak volumes. Oh, Jillian, this is wonderful. Just how serious is your relationship with Forrest?"

"Whoa." Jillian leaned toward her. "There is *no* relationship, Deedee. He's The Project, remember?"

"Well, just because it started out like that doesn't mean—"

"Yes, it does," Jillian interrupted. "I don't want any part of a serious relationship. No commitment. Forrest is very aware of that."

"You've talked about it?"

"It's come up in conversation. I'm concentrating on reprogramming his mind about working too hard. That's what you and Andrea wanted me to do."

"Yes, we did. Yes, of course. But, Jillian, I know you. You don't engage in casual sex. Therefore, there are emotions involved...respect, caring, sharing. Correct?"

"Well, I... Yes, okay, correct."

"Then how can you say you're not in a relationship with him? What button do you push to turn those emotions off at the end of your vacation? My darling friend, you're scaring me to death. Andrea and I were hoping that— Oh, Jillian, I don't want to see you get hurt. I don't want to see Forrest get hurt."

"It won't happen. Trust me. So, yes, all right, things are sort of intense between us, and there *are* emotions involved, but Forrest and I realize we're poles apart in what we want in life. At the end of my vacation, I'll go back to work, and Forrest will ride off into the sunset. Meaning he'll go back to work, too. *No one is going to get hurt.*"

"Would you ladies care for some dessert?" the waitress asked, appearing at the table.

"An aspirin," Deedee said, pressing one hand against her forehead. "I have a roaring, stress headache."

"Oh, good grief," Jillian muttered, rolling her eyes heavenward.

Hours later, Jillian stood in front of the full-length mirror in her bedroom, straightening a new bright-red sweater over the waistband of her jeans.

Forrest had suggested an evening at his apartment spent watching movies on the VCR and eating tons of buttery popcorn.

Fun, Jillian mused as she left the bedroom, and lazily perfect, due to the fact that she was exhausted from the afternoon of shopping. Deedee, thank goodness, had not brought up the subject of Forrest or The Project again, and they'd thoroughly enjoyed their spending spree.

Jillian had nodded in approval as she hung each purchase in the closet after staggering in with an armload of boxes and bags.

She and Forrest had agreed with no argument that they'd watch classic mysteries. Forrest was going to rent a stack on the way to pick her up, and all was well.

Just as Jillian came into the entry hall, the doorbell rang, producing an instant smile on her face. She opened the door, and Forrest entered, pushing the door closed with his foot. He took Jillian into his arms and kissed her.

Oh, yes, she thought dreamily, returning his ardor with total abandon. Hello, Forrest MacAllister.

The kiss deepened.

No one is going to get hurt.

The words she'd spoken with such conviction at lunch suddenly slammed against her mind.

Darn that Deedee, Jillian thought. She'd planted that niggling little seed of doubt. No. She wasn't going to fall prey to Deedee's lovable-but-unnecessary concern. She and Forrest were on the same wavelength regarding their relationship and knew it was *not* a relationship.

Forrest lifted his head. "Hello, Jillian. I missed you."

"You what?" she said, her eyes widening.

He released her and crossed his arms over his chest. "I missed you. I thought about you all day."

"Oh, well, that's nice," she said, managing a weak smile.

He'd missed her? Well, that was no big deal. She'd missed him, too, she supposed. When a person was looking forward to an event, they missed not being part of that event when it wasn't time yet for the event to begin. Did that make sense? Oh, heavens, she was scrambling her brain.

"Let's go," she said. "I have a craving for popcorn."

During the drive to his apartment, Forrest told Jillian he'd finished reading another of her novels. Jillian inwardly groaned, knowing there would be no way to keep him from talking at length about the book. She *really* didn't want to think about her work tonight, as it was connected to her vacation, which was connected to The Project. Oh, blast.

"The message is there again in the book," Forrest said. "Truth, trust. The hero courts the heroine, she agrees to marry him, off they go on their wedding trip in his fancy coach.

"But, shame on them, they've been keeping the truth from each other. He has to have an heir under the terms of his grandfather's will, and she needs money to pay back-taxes on the family home where her widowed mother and four siblings live. She figures she can squirrel away bucks from her wifely allowance."

"Yes, I know, Forrest," Jillian said wearily. "I wrote it."

"Time passes," he went on, as though she hadn't spoken, "and, bingo, they fall in love. But due to the wagging tongues of the *ton*, they discover the truth about why each married the other. They feel betrayed and used. Hell, they've *really hurt* the person they now love."

"Not exactly *really hurt*," Jillian said. "I mean, okay, they were hurt, but not *really hurt*, with the emphasis you're putting on it. You make it sound as though they're bleeding to death."

"They are, in a way," he said, nodding. "They're emotionally bleeding. You, as the writer, made me feel their pain. Those two were in a world of hurt, Jillian."

"Don't say that," she snapped, then sighed. "I'm sorry. I didn't mean to bark at you. I guess I'm a little frazzled because I've been on the go all day. Once I put my feet up, relax, and start watching a movie, I'll be fine."

"And have popcorn," he said, smiling over at her.

"Yes, oodles of popcorn," she agreed absently.

No one is going to get hurt.

Oh, Jillian, please, she begged herself, shut up.

* * *

Two hours later, Forrest left the kitchen with another big bowl of popcorn, then stopped in the doorway of the living room.

He looked at Jillian curled up in the corner of his extra-long sofa, her eyes riveted on the television screen. His gaze swept over the room.

Jillian had said she liked his apartment and he had no reason to doubt her sincerity. He'd decorated in earth tones of brown, tan, and oatmeal, with accents of orange and yellow. The furniture was heavy, dark wood, giving the room a definite masculine aura.

There had been countless women in this room during the past, coming in and going out. But this was the first time he was so acutely aware that it felt incredibly *right* to have a woman in his home. Not just any woman—Jillian.

He had, to his own amazement and chagrin, counted down the hours of the seemingly endless day until finally it was time to pick up Jillian.

Since he'd awakened that morning her image had hovered constantly in his mind's eye. It was so vivid he felt he could reach out and gather her into his arms. When she'd opened the door of her house, he'd registered a sense of completeness, a mental sigh of relief that he was once again with Jillian.

MacAllister, he thought, get it together. Jillian was his Angels and Elves assignment, and he wasn't doing particularly well in changing her mind-set about work. He was caught up in the magic spell of the woman, instead of concentrating on the mission at hand.

Well, hell, that was easy to understand. Jillian was fantastic. She was intelligent, fascinating, fun, and had a great sense of humor. And when they made love, it was like nothing he'd experienced before. It was as though they were meshing their hearts, minds and souls, as well as their bodies.

But he *knew* they were looking for different things from life. Jillian was adamant in her stand that she preferred to live alone, just as she was doing. The problem was, he just knew that she would view the future differently if she could put the ghosts of her past to rest.

Forrest frowned as he continued to stare at Jillian.

One of Jillian's major concerns had come across loud and clear in each of her novels he'd read so far—the importance of trust. That message was Jillian's voice, her beliefs and values. She had trusted him enough to tell him of her lonely childhood. She trusted him with her very essence each time they made love.

But there was a section of herself she protected. She hadn't shared her past pain, or the details of what had destroyed her brief marriage. He needed her to take that final step, he really did.

Before he could completely believe that Jillian wanted a solitary existence, wanted to concentrate almost totally on her work, he had to be convinced that the past wasn't dictating her future.

Why was he so determined that Jillian should trust him enough to reveal her ghosts? Of course, how else could he complete his assignment in the proper Angels and Elves manner if he didn't have all the data he needed? There, that made perfect sense.

"Hooray," Jillian said, clapping her hands. "They solved the mystery. I love it, I love it. The butler did it. Can you believe that, Forrest? The butler actually did it."

Forrest crossed the room and put the fresh batch of popcorn on the coffee table. Sitting down next to Jil-

lian, he pressed the button on the remote control to re-
wind the movie.

"Let's take a break before we watch the next one," he
said. "All right?"

"Sure," she said, reaching for a handful of popcorn.
"You're a terrific popcorn popper, Forrest."

"That's good to know. If things get slow at the office,
I can moonlight as a popcorn popper." He paused.
"What did your husband do for a living?"

Jillian's head snapped up and she frowned as she met
his gaze.

"Where did that come from?" she said, a slight edge
in her voice.

He shrugged. "I was wondering, that's all."

"Why?"

"Because, Jillian, we are today the sum total of all we
have been. You were married, but it didn't work out. It
stands to reason that it was a painful time in your life.
I've learned so much about you since we met. We've
talked for hours. But that section of your life is closed
off, kept behind a protective wall."

"I prefer not to discuss it."

"I realize that, but it leaves a piece of the marvelous
puzzle that is you, now, missing. I don't know if this
makes sense to you, but it's important to me." He continued to look directly into her eyes.

No, it didn't make sense, Jillian thought. Forrest was
talking like a man who was in a committed relationship,
wanting to know all and everything about the woman he
loved. That wasn't remotely close to what they were together. He wanted love, marriage, a family. So what dif-
ference did it make if some of the pieces of Jillian—the
puzzle, as he put it—were missing?

You're not being fair, Jillian, she admonished herself. She'd gathered her data about Forrest, found out what *she* needed to know before declaring him to be The Project. Who was she to stand in judgment of what details were important to him?

But, dear heaven, he was asking so much of her. She'd buried it all so deep, refused to allow the pain to touch her again. If she dragged it all out into the open, she'd feel stripped bare and vulnerable. She would be trusting Forrest with a raw wound that might never totally heal.

"Jillian?" he said quietly. Trust me. Ah, Jillian, please, trust me. "Will you tell me about it?"

She drew a shuddering breath. "Do you have any idea what you're asking of me?"

"Yes. I'm asking you to trust me."

"That's exactly it. That's the issue ... trust."

"And truth, honesty, respect. Do you trust me, Jillian?"

Yes, her mind whispered.

There were no warring voices beating against her, no chilling doubts, no fear. There was simply a warm, peaceful, whispering word: *yes.*

"My husband was more than twenty years older than me," she said, her voice trembling slightly. "He was one of my college professors. Oh, I was so in love, or I believed I was at the time. I've since wondered if I wasn't seeking a father figure because I'd never had a close relationship with mine."

Forrest's heart thundered, and he was hardly breathing.

She was doing it, he mentally cheered. Jillian was trusting him with her innermost secret. She was giving him, at that very moment, a very special gift, and he would cherish it.

"I got pregnant," she said softly. "He...his name was Roger. He whisked me off and married me, moved me into his house, and that was that. It all happened so fast, I hardly had a chance to think. I continued in school, but two months later I lost the baby."

"Ah, Jillian, I'm sorry."

"I was terribly upset, really devastated, because I wanted that baby so very much." Sudden tears filled her eyes, and she blinked them away angrily. "Anyway, Roger shrugged off the miscarriage and refused to address my sorrow. I felt...I felt as alone as I had as a child. There was no one there for me. No one."

"What about your parents?"

"They never knew I was pregnant. I've never told them."

"Dear God, Jillian, why did you do that to yourself?"

"Because I'm the only one I can truly count on to be there for myself," she said, her voice rising. "That's how it is, how it's always been."

"No, I..."

"Yes! Roger continued on with his life as though he'd forgotten he had a wife. I never knew where he was, when he'd be home. Oh, he was attentive and charming when he showed up, but... One day I cut class because I had a bad cold. I came home and there was Roger in bed with a pretty coed. She was that year's model of the adoring student."

Forrest swore under his breath.

"There was an awful scene," Jillian went on. "The girl was hysterical, said she was pregnant with Roger's child, demanded that I let him go so he could marry her, the woman he really loved."

"What did the bastard say?" Forrest said, a muscle twitching in his jaw.

"It would almost have been funny if I hadn't been so shattered. He looked rather bemused, then calmly said that it was best if he married the girl because she was, after all, pregnant with his baby. Surely I understood, as he'd done the same for me. I divorced him."

"Jillian..."

"So, there you have it," she said, lifting her chin. "Why you wanted that ugly puzzle piece, I don't know. I've trusted you with the whole nasty story, Forrest. I was young, naive and gullible. I was also very stupid. But I learned from that experience. Oh, yes, I certainly learned a great deal."

Forrest moved closer to her and framed her face in his hands. "I'm sorry you went through that nightmare, Jillian. I'd turn back the clock and change history for you if I could, but I can't. All I can do is thank you for trusting me with your pain. I mean that sincerely. Thank you."

"Well, it should make it clear to you why I don't want any part of marriage ever again. *Not ever.* I'm doing just fine with my life the way it's structured now. *I* don't need to implement any of the compromises I spoke of so that I don't have to work so hard. I like my schedule just as it is. You're the one who is due to make adjustments so you can have the family you want.

"We're doing fine, Forrest, you and I together, because we understand each other, and we realize that we simply want different things in the future. But for now, there's no problem."

Wrong, Forrest thought, capturing her lips with his. There was definitely a problem. Jillian's dragons from the past had to be slain before she could be free to have a future made up of more than just work.

His Angels and Elves assignment was becoming much more complicated than he'd anticipated, but he could handle it. He had to—for Jillian. It had nothing to do with him, really; Jillian deserved to have more in her life than she was allowing herself.

No, of course it didn't have anything to do with him, personally.

He was simply going to see his Angels and Elves assignment through to its proper end.

Eight

Early the next afternoon, Forrest telephoned Jillian to say he had to make an unexpected trip up the coast to San Francisco. The woman who had replaced Andrea at MacAllister Architects was to have made a presentation to a group of investors planning to build a large apartment complex. The woman was sick in bed with the flu, and Forrest was going in her place.

"Oh, I see," Jillian said, acutely aware of the wave of disappointment that swept through her.

Forrest chuckled. "Now don't start in on me about working while I'm supposed to be taking time off. This is a red-alert emergency."

"I understand that, I really do. How long will you be gone?"

"If everything goes as planned, I'll be back Wednesday afternoon. This is Monday, so...yes, I should be able to wind it up by then." He paused. "I'll miss you, Jillian. That sounds too lightweight for how I'm feeling. I will *really* miss you."

"I'll miss you, too. Listen, why don't I cook dinner for us Wednesday night? Don't expect fancy, because the few things I can make are very basic. I haven't poisoned myself so far, though."

"That's comforting," he said, laughing. "I accept your invitation to dinner. Take good care of yourself, Lady Jillian, and I'll see you as soon as I possibly can. Bye for now."

"Goodbye, Forrest," she said, then replaced the receiver slowly, staring at it for a long moment before she moved away.

She wandered into the living room, sat down on the sofa, then got up again, too restless to sit still.

She felt rather... empty, she realized. As a writer she was accustomed to keeping her own company. It was emphasized at every writers' conference she'd ever attended that writing was a lonely profession, requiring the person to spend countless hours alone in order to achieve her goals. She had no problem with that. She liked herself, and the comfortable haven of her home.

No, she'd had no difficulty with the isolation of being an author.

Until now.

Until Forrest.

"Perdition." She halted her trek and pressed her hands to her cheeks.

What was happening to her? What was Forrest MacAllister doing to her?

She still found it hard to believe that she'd actually told Forrest the grim details of her disastrous marriage. She'd opened her mouth and the story had just spilled out. The unsettling part was that it had felt right, so good, to share it with him, and in the light of this new day she wasn't one bit sorry that she had. Why?

Jillian threw up her hands and continued to pace around the living room.

She didn't want Forrest to go to San Francisco. She wanted him here, with her. She didn't want to be alone, she wanted to be with Forrest. She didn't want to have to wait until Wednesday night to see him, she wanted to see him right now.

Oh, dear heaven, what did it all mean?

Jillian ordered herself to calm down. She needed to gather her data. She was on vacation, and during any other hiatus would be filling her idle hours with The Project. Since Forrest was The Project, it was perfectly reasonable that she would miss him, would feel incomplete because he wasn't there, and would be a tad lonely.

Thank goodness, she'd figured it out. For a moment there she'd panicked, thought perhaps her emotions had run roughshod over her common sense. Thought perhaps she'd done something as foolish as falling in love with Forrest MacAllister.

Well, that wasn't the case. She was under control, doing fine. She'd have to improvise for a couple of days, come up with miniprojects to tide her over until Forrest returned and resumed his role of The Project.

She would read, watch movies, plan the menu for Wednesday night's dinner, then shop for the necessary groceries. She'd polish her fingernails, write a letter to her parents, go to Deedee's store and spend oodles of money on books, and wash her car.

All of that sounded as thrilling as having a root canal.

She wanted to be with Forrest!

"Jillian," she said, a warning tone in her voice, "knock it off, shape up, get it together. Now!"

* * *

Forrest once again found Andrea propped up against pillows on the sofa in her living room, her nose buried in a book. This time, however, his arrival produced a stormy glare from his sister, rather than a sunny smile.

"Having a bad hair day?" Forrest said pleasantly, sitting down in a chair he pulled next to the sofa.

"You've been avoiding me, Forrest MacAllister," Andrea said. "You haven't returned any of the messages I've left on your answering machine."

"I'm a busy man. I have places to go, people to see. I'm out of here in a minute, and on my way to San Francisco. But I came by to tell you not to have the twins while I'm gone because I'd miss out on The Baby Bet, and that would *not* please me. I'm the current champion of The Baby Bet, and I have my title to protect."

"You'd better protect your nose," she said, glowering, "because I feel like punching it. If it wasn't for Deedee, I wouldn't know that you're dating Jillian. You made her your Angels and Elves assignment and didn't even tell me, you rat."

Forrest snapped his fingers. "Slipped my mind."

"Forrest," Andrea said warningly.

"Don't stress, Andrea. It's not good for the munchkins. I didn't tell you because you'd want details, details, details."

"Of course, silly man, how else am I to know what's happening?" She folded her hands over her enormous stomach. "Now then, tell all."

Forrest got to his feet. "Can't. Have to hit the road." He kissed her on the forehead. "Bye." He spun around and strode from the room.

"Oh, dear," Andrea said to the empty room, "what have Deedee and I done? She's afraid someone is going to end up with a broken heart because of this fiasco." She patted her stomach. "Your mommy should never have played Cupid, little ones. I'm going to feel terrible if Forrest or Jillian get hurt. Oh, dear, dear, dear."

Late that night, Forrest lay in bed in his hotel room in San Francisco, his hands laced beneath his head as he stared at the ceiling.

He'd called Jillian earlier and they'd had a nice chat. She'd sounded chipper, had told him that the day had flown by as she'd filled the hours with one activity after another, including washing her car. She missed him, of course, and hoped his trip would be a huge success. She'd see him Wednesday evening, and had said, "Good night, Forrest."

He had fully expected to drop off to sleep immediately after speaking with Jillian, but three hours had gone by and blissful slumber was remaining annoyingly elusive.

Jillian, Jillian, Jillian, he mused. He replayed the sad tale of her marriage, hearing the trembling of her voice, seeing the flickers of sorrow and pain in her expressive gray eyes.

He'd been consumed with rage directed toward the unfeeling Roger, and had registered the urge to track the jerk down and wring his insensitive neck.

It meant a lot to him, it really did, that Jillian had trusted him enough to tell him about her marriage. That trust was a precious gift he intended to cherish as the treasure it was.

So, where did he stand in his Angels and Elves assignment? Well, if by telling him about her past Jillian was able to put the ghosts to rest, then he was doing great.

She would be free to take a fresh look at the structure of her existence and to reevaluate her adamant "No way" regarding marriage and children.

Jillian married? To a man? Having that man's child? Making love with that man to conceive that baby?

"Damn," he said.

He didn't like that idea one iota. The thought of another man touching her, reaching for her in the night... No!

"Cool it, MacAllister," he said to the ceiling.

Okay, he was calm. Fine. The reason the image of some jerk being with Jillian was upsetting him was because *he,* Forrest MacAllister, was presently the one in Jillian's life *and* in her bed. His initial reaction didn't mean he'd gone off the deep end and fallen in love with her.

To fall in love with Jillian would be very, *very* foolish, as there was no guarantee that his Angels and Elves assignment would be a success. She could very well choose to continue her life exactly the way it was.

As for him? Well, he was registering a surge of hope that he just might be able to have the wife and children he yearned for. Jillian's fresh take on the subject was beginning to make sense. Compromise. Maybe, just maybe, his deepest wish could yet come true.

Forrest yawned, and minutes later he drifted off to sleep, dreaming of sailing ships.

Jillian peered into the oven, then closed the door with a loud bang.

"Oh, posh," she said, flinging out her arms. "Why aren't you cooking, chicken? You're just sitting there like a lump." She swept her gaze over the multitude of dials on top of the stove. "Aaak!" she yelled, smacking her hands onto the top of her head. "I didn't turn it on!"

She flipped the appropriate dial with more force than necessary, then burst into laughter.

When it came to cooking, she was a dud. She and Forrest were going to dine fashionably late. No, actually, they were going to dine so late they would be creating a whole new fashion of their own.

Why couldn't she get the hang of this cooking nonsense? It simply called for organization, planning, a sense of order where one thing led to the next. Those were all abilities she possessed whenever she was writing a book, so why didn't that knowledge follow her out of the office and into the kitchen?

"Beats me," she said, with a shrug. "Go for it, chicken," she added, giving the top of the stove a friendly pat.

As she walked toward the kitchen door, she suddenly stopped, a frown replacing her smile. With a sense of dread, she turned slowly to stare at the calendar that hung on the wall next to the telephone.

Time was passing so quickly, she thought, wrapping her hands around her elbows. There was less than a week left of her vacation, less than a week to be with Forrest.

She edged closer to the calendar, her eyes riveted on the numbered squares. A chill swept through her, causing her to tighten her hold on her arms.

In her mental vision, she saw herself in her large office, pouring over the multitude of reference books, making notes, carefully plotting her next novel. It was a familiar picture, as that room was where she spent the vast majority of her life.

And it suddenly appeared very empty, and very, *very* lonely.

"No," she whispered, feeling the ache of threatening tears in her throat, "no, it isn't lonely. It's my world. It's where I belong, where I'm content. Safe." She took a shuddering breath.

On trembling legs she went to the table, sinking onto one of the chairs.

In her mind's eye she saw Forrest—smiling, talking, then looking at her with an intense message of desire radiating from his beautiful brown eyes. Heat swirled within her as she relived the lovemaking they'd shared; her breasts grew heavy, aching for the exquisite touch of Forrest's hands, the sensuality of his mouth savoring her soft flesh.

She saw him in her bed, naked and bronzed; so powerful, his strength tempered with infinite gentleness. She saw him in the shower, in the kitchen making coffee, eating pizza in front of the roaring fire in the hearth. She saw him in the ballroom where they'd danced, then decked out in Western clothes at the concert, and at the helm of the cabin cruiser.

Then she saw him walking away, out of her life, not looking back as he left.

"Oh, Forrest, please, no," she said, tears misting her eyes.

In the next instant, she got to her feet, lifted her chin, and stomped out of the kitchen.

She was being ridiculous, she fumed, heading for her bedroom. She *knew* Forrest was in her life temporarily. He was The Project, for heaven's sake. The Project was always over at the end of her two-week vacation. Just because he had the added title of being an Angels and Elves assignment, didn't mean the time allowed would be extended.

There was less than one week left to be with Forrest.

She knew that.

"So, get a grip, Jillian," she told herself. "You're behaving like an idiot."

Yes, she cared for Forrest, she truly did, and she would miss him for a while after he was gone. But she wasn't in love with him, for crying out loud. She wouldn't do something as stupid as falling in love with the man. No, absolutely not.

In her room she changed clothes, donning a full-length Indian-print caftan she'd bought during her shopping spree with Deedee. After brushing her hair, she checked her makeup, sprayed on a floral cologne, then sank onto the side of the bed.

Shadows from the past suddenly crept over her, encasing her in a dark cocoon of memories that began to take the form of hideous, near-human entities, each with a name.

Pain. Betrayal. Disillusionment. Vulnerability. Abandonment. Loneliness.

They were all there, taunting her with hollow, cruel voices that grew louder in a maddening cadence. They were spawned by love, by loving, by having placed her heart in the hands of another.

No! She wouldn't do it, not ever again! There was no way on earth that she would allow herself to fall in love with Forrest. He would not be given that kind of power and control.

Her work, her writing, was her focus and the essence of who she was. It required her complete attention and dedication. There wasn't room for anything else. No space for distractions or temptations that would lure her away and destroy the career to which she'd dedicated herself.

The doorbell chimed, and Jillian jerked in surprise at the sudden intrusion into her tangled thoughts. She went to the mirror, scrutinizing herself critically for any signs of turmoil or stress that would cause Forrest to question her.

She appeared perfectly normal, she decided, then hurried from the room.

The bell rang again before Jillian reached the entryway, and she quickened her step even more. When she opened the door, all rational thought fled.

"Forrest," she whispered.

"Jillian."

Forrest closed the door behind him, then swept her into his arms, his mouth capturing hers, parting her lips; his tongue seeking and finding hers in the sweet darkness.

Jillian flung her arms around his neck and molded her body to his, returning in kind the hungry, urgent force of the kiss. Her breasts were crushed to the hard wall of his chest, and she felt and savored the pressure of his arousal, heavy against her.

This was Forrest, her mind hummed. Forrest was here. She'd missed him terribly, and was so very glad he was back.

Forrest lifted his head to meet her gaze, but didn't release her. He drew a rough breath before he attempted to speak.

"Lord, I missed you," he said, then brushed his lips over hers.

"I missed you, too."

"I swear, Jillian, never before have floor plans, bathroom designs and square footage seemed like such ridiculous subjects to be pitching to a roomful of megabucks boys. All I could think about was getting out of there and coming home to you."

Jillian's heart skipped a beat.

Coming home to you.

Home.

Jillian, don't, she admonished herself. Forrest hadn't meant that the way it sounded. This was *her* home, not his, not theirs. This was where she lived—alone.

"Did you get the job?" she asked.

"Yep. The contract is signed, sealed, and delivered." He stared into space and sniffed the air. "Either you have a new and unusual cologne, or I smell the delicious scent of baking chicken."

Jillian laughed and stepped back, instantly wishing she was still nestled close to him.

"The aroma of that chicken is all you're going to get for a while," she said, smiling. "I'm officially declaring myself a disaster as a cook. I forgot to turn on the oven. We're going to dine—check that fancy jargon—very late. Come in by the fire. I can at least offer you a drink and some cheese and crackers."

"Sold," he said, putting one arm around her shoulders. "I really like that dress you're wearing. I suppose it has a fancier title than 'dress.'"

"Close enough," she said, as they went into the living room. "You're rather spiffy yourself, sir."

He was gorgeous, she mused. Wearing black slacks and a burgundy sweater that was the exact shade of one of the multitude of colors in her caftan, Forrest looked fabulous. *They* looked fabulous, together.

"Wine, cheese, and crackers?" she said, remaining standing as Forrest sat down on the sofa.

"Great. Do you need some help?"

"No, I'm your official hostess this evening."

"Then you're supposed to say, 'Coffee, tea, or me?' That's the rules of hostessdom."

Jillian laughed as she started toward the kitchen.

Forrest watched her go, filling his senses with the sight of her, her aroma of flowers, the way she'd felt in his arms, the remembrance of the honey-sweet taste of her mouth, the sound of her wind-chime laughter.

Just as Jillian returned carrying a tray, the telephone rang. She hesitated a moment, undecided whether to hurry back to the kitchen, or answer the telephone on the end table by the sofa.

"Would you get that, Forrest?" she finally asked.

He picked up the receiver. "Hello, you've reached the Jones-Jenkins residence."

"Oh, good grief." Jillian rolled her eyes heavenward.

She set the tray on a small table, then moved it in front of the sofa. Looking at Forrest, she frowned as she realized he was ramrod stiff and was now sitting on the edge of the cushion.

"Forrest?" she said. "What is it?"

"You're sure, you're really sure?" he said, into the receiver. "She's had a couple of false alarms, Michael. I know she felt it was different this time. That's why I gave you the telephone number here.... The doctor said that...? Oh, Lord, this is it." He lunged to his feet, nearly yanking the base of the telephone from the table. "You and Jenny are going over there now...? I am *not* repeating everything you say like a damn parrot... Of course, I'm coming. Quit bugging me, will you, so I can get moving!" He slammed the receiver back into place.

"Forrest?" Jillian said again.

"Stay calm, MacAllister," he muttered. "You'll drive into a tree if you don't get it together."

"Forrest MacAllister!" Jillian yelled. "Would you talk to me?"

"Oh," he said, jerking in surprise at her outburst. "Sorry. It's Andrea. She and John are at the hospital, and the doctor says this is it. That was Michael on the phone. The doc said the babies are only a couple of weeks early, so that's good. That's good. Michael and Jenny are leaving for the hospital now." He grabbed Jillian's hand. "Come on. We've got to get over there."

"You want me to come with you?"

He frowned. "Don't you want to?"

"Yes, of course I do, but this is a family event, Forrest. I'm not certain that it would be appropriate for me to intrude. I mean, I'm Andrea's friend, but—"

"Jillian, trust me, it's fine. I imagine Deedee will be there too."

"Well, if you're sure. Let's see. The safety screen is in front of the fire, and— Oh, the chicken. I've got to turn the oven off."

"I'm sorry about the dinner," he said, as she started toward the kitchen.

"Don't be. It wasn't exactly going to be a gourmet delight, anyway. I need to grab a shawl, then we're off and running."

She returned in a few minutes and frowned as she looked at Forrest.

"You're so serious," she said. "Are you worried about Andrea?"

"Yeah, I guess I am. You'd think I'd be cool, considering I've been through this routine with Jenny and Michael. Maybe it's one of those things a person can't ever become casual about. I'd probably pass out cold on my face if it was *my* wife, having *my* baby. Oh, man, I'd never hear the end of that from my family. Okay, let's hit the road."

The drive to the hospital was made in silence as Forrest concentrated on the traffic with more intensity than usual, due to the fact that he was driving far above the speed limit.

Jillian welcomed the mental solitude, using the time to attempt to sift and sort through the maze in her mind.

When Forrest had spoken of *his* wife, having *his* baby, she'd had a vision, to her astonishment and dismay, of that woman being her. As he'd said the words, the image had clicked into place as naturally as breathing. Forcing it away, pushing it from her mind, had not been an easy task.

Why had that happened? She *knew* she didn't wish to ever marry again. She *knew* that. She was also very aware that she had made a career choice that allowed no room for a husband and children.

Well, yes, she was acquainted with many successful authors who combined their writing with a family. But her methods for completing a novel were etched in stone, were the way she had to do it to achieve her goals.

If she made the foolish mistake of falling in love with Forrest MacAllister, it was not going to erase her past or the course she had set for her future.

And that was that.

But as she realized she was about to meet Forrest's entire family and be swept up in the excitement of the soon-to-arrive babies, she wished she'd stayed at home with her stupid, half-baked chicken.

Jillian's apprehensions regarding having accompanied Forrest to the hospital were forgotten within moments of entering the waiting room.

When Forrest introduced her to everyone, she was received with such warmth that she felt as though she'd known the boisterous MacAllister clan for a very long time.

The sons had obviously inherited their height and physiques from their father, Robert, who was still nicely built, with no evidence of a middle-age paunch in sight. His hair was thick and gray, and his smile a delightful carbon copy of Forrest's, Michael's and Ryan's. Ryan's wife, Sherry, was a nurse on duty at another hospital across town.

Margaret MacAllister, Forrest's mother, had a twinkle in her brown eyes, and a smile that lit up her entire face. Her hair was graying, but still had hints of rich auburn, and was attractively styled in a cap of soft curls.

She appeared small and delicate next to the tall, broadshouldered men of her family, but Jillian knew from the enchanting stories Forrest had told her, that Margaret MacAllister was a force to be reckoned with.

Michael's wife, Jenny, was a stunning blonde, who would make heads turn wherever she went. Yet, Jillian realized, Jenny was natural and at ease with her own beauty. Her friendly smile was genuine.

Also present was a smiling Deedee, who waggled her fingers at Jillian from across the room.

Jillian was also introduced to Ted Sharpe, Ryan's partner on the police force. Ted was tall, blond, tanned, and had the bluest eyes Jillian had ever seen. Ryan and Ted, she mentally decided, should pose for police-academy recruiting posters.

Her gaze swept over the group, lingering on the MacAllisters.

This was Forrest's family—a *real* family, the kind she'd fantasized about having during the years she was a lonely child. They'd all gathered together as a supportive unit for Andrea and John. The babies who would soon come into the world would be received into the embrace of these people, and loved unconditionally for all time.

How blessed they all were. But she could sense, feel, that they all knew that.

"Sit, sit," Margaret said, flapping her hands. "Our little darlings aren't going to be born any quicker by us standing around."

Everyone immediately sat down, causing Jillian to smile as she witnessed Margaret in action.

"I'm taking the bets, Forrest," Michael said. "I've got it covered. Two girls, two boys, one of each, girl born first, boy born first, firstborn weighs more, second born weighs more. Take your pick, and give me twenty bucks."

"Don't rush me, here. As The Baby Bet champion, I intend to give this the serious consideration it deserves." Forrest stared at the ceiling. A few minutes later, he took out his wallet and handed Michael the money. "Boy and a girl. Boy first and weighs more."

Michael wrote on a piece of paper. "Got it."

"Enjoy your champion status while you have it, Forrest," Ted said. "I'm going to clean your clock. Two boys. Second one is heavier."

"Dream on, Sharpe," Forrest said, grinning. "You are looking at the pro." He paused. "Anyone seen John? How's the daddy-to-be holding up?"

"Nope, haven't seen him," Robert said. "He's in the labor room with Andrea. He plans on being in the delivery room, too. We weren't allowed to do that in my day. Thank goodness."

Margaret patted her husband's knee. "You could have handled it, dear."

"That's not a bet I would have put twenty dollars on," Robert said, chuckling. "Well, I'm glad John is with our little girl. Andrea may be John's wife, but she'll always be my baby daughter, too."

"Of course she is," Margaret said, then kissed him on the cheek. "That's just the way it is."

Not for everyone, Jillian thought. No, not for everyone.

"I enjoy your books immensely, Jillian," Margaret said. "I can't even imagine how hard you must work to produce a novel. The image of an author most of us have is a life of glitz and glamour, fame and fortune. I have a feeling it's just honest, hard work."

"Yes," Jillian said, looking at her in surprise, "it is. It takes a great deal of self-discipline and many, many hours of solitude."

"Solitude?" Jenny said, laughing. "I vaguely remember that. When you're chasing a toddler all day, solitude is hard to come by. Our Bobby is a busy boy."

The conversation continued with Michael relating the latest activities of his and Jenny's son, Robert, commenting on the fact that Bobby was brilliant beyond his years, and Forrest saying that Bobby inherited his intelligence from Jenny.

Jillian only half listened, as her own words spoken a few minutes before beat against her mind.

Solitude.

It was a given, an understood element in her life that made it possible for her to continue to produce her books on schedule. She didn't question it, nor resent it. For many years now, it had been a fact, a part of her day-to-day existence.

But on this night, sitting there surrounded by the MacAllisters and their friends, with Forrest's arm around her shoulders, the word *solitude* was taking on new and ominous connotations. It seemed to be growing steadily, as though it was suddenly a living entity, getting bigger and darker like a threatening force.

As it grew it took on a new identity.

Its name was Loneliness.

Jillian shivered.

"Are you cold?" Forrest said. "Would you like me to put your shawl around you?"

"What? Oh, no, I'm fine," she said, managing to smile.

"I'm hungry," Michael said.

"You're always hungry," Jenny said.

"Amen to that," Robert said. "I hope for the sake of your budget that Bobby didn't inherit your appetite."

"He did," Michael said. "I need a raise."

"Forget it," Forrest said. "Ryan, I assume you called Sherry?"

"Yep," Ryan said. "They'll page her when I have something to report. She sure would like to be here, though."

"Well, it just can't be helped," Margaret said. "The whole family is here in spirit, and Andrea and John know that."

Dear heaven, Jillian thought, she was going to cry in a minute if she didn't get herself together. She'd just never been a part of anything like this—not in her entire life. It was so beautiful, so incredibly beautiful.

A nurse entered the room and everyone got quickly to their feet.

"Just an update, folks," the nurse said. "We're on our way to the delivery room. Those little ones are eager to greet the world. Andrea is doing splendidly. John is a bit gray around the edges, but he's hanging right in there. It won't be long now." She hurried out of the room.

"Lord—" Forrest pressed one hand to his stomach "—this stuff is so damn scary."

"Oh, yeah?" Michael said. "Wait until you're the one in the weird green clothes, taking part up close and personal. That, my little brother, is terror in its purest form."

Forrest nodded. "Yes, I bet it is, but I'd be there every step of the way." He tightened his hold on Jillian's shoulders. "Count on it."

Nine

—

Forrest won The Baby Bet.

When John appeared in the waiting room in his green garb, Jillian instantly cataloged him in her mind as being tall, good-looking, and very proud. The smile that lit up his face erased the fatigue and strain that had been visible when he first entered the room.

"A boy," he said, beaming, "and a girl. Andrea was fantastic. Absolutely fantastic. She was a lot braver than I was, I can tell you that. She's fine. Exhausted but happy."

"Halt!" Michael said. "Who was born first? Your son, or your daughter?"

"Our son," John said, obviously confused by the question. "Why?"

Michael consulted the piece of paper he held in his hand. "Check. Okay, how much did they weigh?"

"Oh, I get it," John said. "You're doing The Baby Bet bit. Let's see, Forrest is the current champion. Right? Well, here goes. John Matthew, to be called Matt to avoid the two Johns mix-ups, weighed five pounds, eight ounces. Andrea Noel, to be called Noel because Christmas is a very special family celebration, and to avoid the two Andreas mix-ups—"

"John!" Michael said.

"Weighed five pounds," he said, then paused and frowned. "Does my memory fail me?"

"Not if you want to live to tell about it," Michael said. John chuckled. "Four ounces."

"Yes!" Forrest punched one fist in the air. "I'm still The Baby Bet champion. Man, I'm so great at this, it blows my mind. Pay," he added, waggling his fingers as he extended his hand to Michael.

"Damn." Michael slapped the money into Forrest's hand. "Twice in a row. It's a good thing I know this stuff can't be set up ahead of time."

"Now that that's out of the way," Margaret said, "I intend to hug the new daddy. Come here, John. Robert and I are so thrilled."

"You're sure Andrea's fine?" Robert said, as Margaret hugged John.

"She's great," John said. "She'll be taken to her room in a few minutes."

Jenny hugged John. Then Forrest, Michael, Ryan and Ted shook his hand.

"John," Forrest said, "this is Jillian Jones-Jenkins. She came along to keep me calm, cool and collected through this harrowing ordeal."

"Hello, John," Jillian said, smiling, "and congratulations to you and Andrea. A son and a daughter. What a wonderful family you have."

"Thank you," John said. "I don't think I can really express how I'm feeling right now. It's just...well, bigger than I can find words to explain." He cocked his head slightly. "Words. You're Andrea's writer friend. I thought you looked familiar. I've seen your photograph on the back of a whole stack of your books that Andrea has. She's been wanting me to meet you. Hey, I'll be able to tell the twins that a famous writer was here the night they were born."

Jillian laughed. "Well, the 'famous' is stretching it a bit."

"No, it's not," John said. "The thing is, why are you with a dud like Forrest?"

"I was wondering about that myself," Ted said thoughtfully.

"Now, wait just a damn minute," Forrest said.

"Hush, all of you," Margaret said. "Don't get started on your usual nonsense. What I want to know is when we can see the babies?"

"And Andrea," Robert said. "I want to say hello to my girl."

"I'm sorry, Robert," John said, "but you can't see Andrea tonight. Once she's settled in her room, they said I could come in for two seconds to kiss her good-night, but then she's supposed to sleep. As for the babies, I'll go check." He spun around and left the room.

Ryan slid a quick glance at his mother, then leaned toward Jillian. "Forrest really *is* a dud, Jillian," he whispered.

"Ryan Robert," Margaret said, "this is not the time or place to discuss the fact that Forrest is a dud."

"You're agreeing with him?" Forrest said. "What kind of a mother are you? I am *not* a dud."

"Of course, you're not," she said, patting him on the cheek.

"Mothers are prejudiced," Robert said.

"Jillian," Forrest said, "the next time you count your blessings, put being an only child at the very top of your list."

Everyone laughed, then stared at the doorway, watching for John's return.

Oh, she adored this family, Jillian mused. There was so much love and warmth weaving back and forth between them. A stranger passing by that room and hearing the banter might draw the conclusion that these people were at odds with each other and someone was close to being decked.

But she knew better as she stood in their midst. They were wonderful. No, being an only child wasn't one of her blessings to be counted.

"Ladies and gentlemen and Forrest," John announced from the doorway, "John Matthew and Andrea Noel are now receiving visitors. Follow me."

As they all went down the hallway, Jillian felt the increased tempo of her heart as she eagerly anticipated her first glimpse of the twins.

She had not, she realized, ever seen a newborn baby up close. When she'd visited friends to take a gift for a new addition, she'd always waited several weeks before going, having decided there was enough confusion in that household early on.

Andrea and John's babies were not even an hour old. What would they look like? Would they be sleeping? Crying? Would they—

Suddenly, there they were.

Behind a large window, a nurse stood close to the glass, a pink blanket-wrapped bundle tucked in the crook of one arm, a blue bundle in the other. A buzz of comments erupted from the group, but Jillian heard only a faint hum of voices far in the distance.

Her gaze was riveted on the babies. They both had skin the shade of a peach at perfection, and caps of silky, auburn hair. Matthew was crying, his tiny fists flailing in the air, emphasizing his displeasure over an unknown something. Noel was sleeping, delicate lashes fanning her cheeks.

Dear heaven, Jillian thought, aware of threatening tears, they were beautiful. They were miracles. Oh, how she wanted to reach out her arms and hold them, cuddle them, feel their little bodies nestled against her breasts.

It had been so many years since she'd allowed herself to think about the baby she'd lost. She'd buried the pain, the sense of emptiness, deep within her, refusing to acknowledge it. Along with Roger's betrayal, she'd refused to address her yearning for the child who had never been born.

But now? There was nowhere to hide from the memories. A baby. Oh, God, she wanted a baby. She wanted to have *Forrest's* baby.

"Jillian?" Forrest said quietly. "Hey, are you all right?"

"What?" She snapped her head up to look at him. "Oh, yes, of course, I'm fine. It's just that... What I mean is..." She tore her gaze from Forrest's and turned to John. "They're wonderful, John, absolutely beautiful."

"Yes," he said, then was unable to speak further as he was overcome with emotion.

Forrest frowned as he stared at Jillian.

What was she thinking? he wondered. What was going on in that complicated, fascinating mind of hers? He sure as hell knew what *he* was thinking. He wanted to marry Jillian Jones-Jenkins *now*, make a commitment with her and to her *now*, create the miracle that would be their child *now*. He wanted it all.

Because he was in love with Jillian Jones-Jenkins.

During the drive back to Jillian's, for reasons he himself didn't understand, Forrest chattered nonstop, relating the tale of how Andrea had met John.

Forrest and Andrea were to have a luncheon meeting with a prospective client, John, who was in need of landscaping for a rental property he had purchased as an investment. He also wished to have an addition built onto the house to increase its value. He was considering hiring MacAllister Architects, since they were equipped to handle both of his needs.

Forrest had drawn up plans for the new room, and Andrea had prepared several proposals for the landscaping. Andrea and Forrest were to arrive at the restaurant in separate vehicles because Andrea had an earlier appointment.

Everything was fine and dandy, Forrest went on, except for the fact that it was raining cats and dogs. He'd met John at the designated time, but there was no sign of Andrea.

"Where was she?" Jillian said, having to force herself to pay attention to the tale.

"Changing a flat tire. Oh, man, you should have seen her when she came into that swanky restaurant." He chuckled and shook his head at the remembered images. "She was soaked to the skin, splattered with mud, and her shoes were squishing with every sloppy step she took. She looked like a drowned rat, a total wreck. Lord, she was a mess. Believe me, if I had known the word at the time, I would have yelled 'Perdition!' at the top of my lungs."

"Oh, my goodness," Jillian said, smiling. "Then what happened?"

"Andrea," Forrest related, "sat down just as calm as you please and made her presentation as though there wasn't a thing wrong with her appearance. She simply ignored the sound of the water from her clothes dripping steadily onto the floor with a maddening cadence. John was not only impressed with Andrea's expertise as a landscape architect, but also with Andrea, herself, and her unbelievable performance. True love, as well as landscaping, was in bloom.

"And they're in the process of living happily ever after," Forrest said. "Yep, just like in one of your books."

He slid a quick glance at Jillian. Lord, how he loved her. He was honest-to-goodness in love! He was, he guessed, talking a blue streak because his mind was a mess, a tangled maze. He was in love for the first time in his life, and he had no idea if he was ecstatic or terrified.

Why? Because he didn't know if Jillian loved *him*. Oh, man, he was heading for a nervous breakdown, no doubt about it.

"Jenny and Michael are happy little lovebirds, too," he blathered on. "As a matter of fact, so are Sherry and Ryan, *and* my parents. Yes, sir, there's a lot of that happy-ending stuff going around in the *real* world, as well as in your novels."

"Your family," Jillian said quietly, "is a lovely exception to the general rule."

"No, I don't believe that, Jillian. The gloom-and-doomers get a charge out of spouting endless statistics about the soaring divorce rate, but there are a multitude of happily married people in this world."

Easy, MacAllister, he mentally warned himself. Be very careful.

"I realize that you had a marriage that caused you a great deal of pain and disillusionment, Jillian, but that's all in the past. If you allow it to determine your attitude in the present, you could miss out on something rare, something special. Know what I mean?"

As Forrest spoke, dark visions from the past flashed before Jillian's eyes, causing a chill to shimmer through her.

Forrest was preaching at her, she thought angrily, about something of which he knew nothing. How easy it was for someone who had never experienced the horror of betrayal, of divorce, to say 'Hey, forget it. That was then, this is now. Go for the gusto in the present.' Well, it wasn't that simple, damn it.

Besides, even if she *had* managed to escape from the painful ghosts, it wouldn't erase the fact that her work was her focus now. She didn't have time for romance, a committed relationship, a husband and family.

But, oh, those babies, those beautiful, precious twins. Such yearning they'd evoked in her, such aching desire to have a child, Forrest's child. A baby fathered by the man she loved with every breath in her body.

Jillian blinked. What? The man she what? Oh, no. No, no, no. She was in love with Forrest MacAllister? How could she have allowed that to happen? She didn't want to be in love. But she was. Oh, yes, she was deeply in love with Forrest.

"Hello?" Forrest said. "Are you awake over there?"

"What? Oh, I was thinking that I might dedicate my next book to the twins, because I feel very honored to have been there tonight when they were born."

Perdition! Forrest fumed. He hadn't even dented Jillian's protective walls with his gushing report of marital bliss and happy endings. Jillian's dragons were mighty tough dudes to slay.

"Gear up, MacAllister," he muttered.

"Pardon me?"

"Nothing. There's your house up ahead. We have the sad task awaiting us of pronouncing your chicken officially dead."

Jillian stared at the house as they drove closer, then turned into the driveway.

Her haven, her safe place, suddenly appeared too big, too empty. In a few short days, she would be back in her office working—alone. She'd spend the nights—alone. She'd exist in the world she'd created for herself—alone. Without Forrest. Oh, dear heaven, without Forrest MacAllister.

When they entered the house, a wave of despair and loneliness swept through Jillian with such bone-chilling intensity that she staggered slightly from the impact. She flung herself into Forrest's arms. He instinctively wrapped his arms around her, surprise evident on his face.

"Make love to me, Forrest," Jillian said, her voice trembling. "Please."

He frowned. "That's not a request I'm about to deny, but... Jillian, what's wrong? You're obviously upset about something. Let's talk about it. Okay?"

"No. No, I don't want to talk."

As Forrest opened his mouth to protest further, Jillian stood on tiptoe and captured his lips with her own, her tongue delving into his mouth to seek and find his. She molded her body to his, crushing her breasts to his chest, feeling his arousal surge against her.

She didn't want to talk, her mind hammered. She didn't want to think. She wished only to feel, fill her senses and the essence of herself with Forrest, savoring all that he was.

Forrest had a fleeting image in his mind of noble Roman tapping him on the shoulder, telling him that this damsel was in distress, that a serious discussion was in order.

But as Jillian sank her fingers into his hair and urged his mouth harder onto hers, Forrest mentally told Roman to take a flying leap off the highest mast of his sailing ship.

Jillian wanted him, Forrest thought hazily, and heaven knew he wanted her. He was on fire, burning with a desire for her that was never, ever, fully extinguished. It smoldered, waiting to be fanned into leaping flames of passion that consumed him with need.

He tore his lips from Jillian's, lifted her into his arms, and carried her down the hall to her bedroom. Setting her on her feet next to the bed, he snapped on the small lamp on the nightstand, flung back the bed linens, then drew her into his embrace once more.

His mouth melted over hers, and the kiss was searing, nearly rough in its intensity. Tongues met, dueled, danced, stroked in a sensual rhythm. Forrest raised his head only long enough to take a sharp breath, then slanted his mouth the other way, drinking in Jillian's sweet taste. She trembled in his arms.

When he gathered handfuls of the material of her caftan, she broke the kiss and shook her head, taking a step backward.

Forrest frowned for a moment, then understood her intentions as she quickly removed the caftan herself, dropping it to the floor. As she continued to shed her clothing, he removed his own. Their eager hands then reached for each other, and they tumbled onto the bed.

Hands, lips and tongues explored—caressing, kissing, tasting, discovering what they had known before but was now somehow new and wondrous.

Whispers and whimpers and moans of pleasure, accompanied by the tantalizing pain of need, escaped from their lips, neither knowing which of them had made the passion-laden sounds.

As Forrest drew the soft flesh of one of her breasts deep into his mouth, Jillian gripped his shoulders tightly, closing her eyes to focus inwardly, not wishing to miss one precious sensation, one lick of the heated flames sweeping through her. The steady pull of Forrest's mouth on her breast was matched by a pulsing tempo deep within her.

He left her breast to reclaim her mouth, then moved over her at last, entering her, thrusting fully into her, bringing to her all that he was.

She gasped as he suddenly slid his arms around her back and rolled over, taking her with him. She moved slowly, tentatively upward, her hands sliding through the moist curls on his muscled chest, her knees on either side of his narrow hips.

Their eyes met, mirroring desire in smoky hues, and then the rhythm began. Forrest grasped her waist, nearly encircling it with his large hands, raising his body to meet each pounding motion.

Exquisite tension coiled within them, tighter and hotter, bringing them closer and closer to the final ecstasy. They each held back by sheer force of will; waiting, anticipating.

And then . . .

"Forrest!"

Jillian threw her head back, calling his name again, then yet again. He lifted his hips one last time and found his own release, a moan rumbling deep in his chest. Each wave of sensation that rocketed through them carried them higher, delivering them to a glorious place where they could only travel together.

A soft sob escaped from Jillian's lips, then she fell forward to be caught tightly against Forrest's chest by his waiting arms. She shifted her legs to the tops of his, and buried her face in the crook of his neck.

Neither spoke. The haze slowly dissipated as their heated bodies cooled and heartbeats quieted.

"Jillian," Forrest finally said, his voice still gritty with passion.

"Hmm?" she said, not moving.

"I love you."

As he felt Jillian stiffen in his arms, Forrest silently cursed, calling himself seven kinds of fool for allowing his emotions to override his good sense.

But in the next moment, he was aware and surprised as his anger shifted in another direction.

Damn it, he thought, he was the other half of this pair, of Jillian Jones-Jenkins and Forrest MacAllister, together. He had wants, needs, emotions. He had dreams and goals. Not everything could, or should, be geared solely to Jillian's mind-set, *her* emotional timetable.

Yes, there were dragons from Jillian's past to slay, but they could fight them together, united as one unbeatable force. There was a time to keep silent, but the moment had come to speak, to declare his love, to be open and honest about the depth of his feelings. Or... or was he making a terrible mistake?

"Jillian?"

"No," she whispered.

Forrest lifted her off him and nestled her close to his side. He placed one finger beneath her chin and lifted her face, forcing her to meet his gaze.

"Listen to me," he said gently.

"Forrest, no, I—"

"Shh," he interrupted. "Please, just hear me out." He paused and moved his hand to her cheek. "I do love you, Jillian. I know without hearing you say the words that my declaration of love frightens you because of what happened to you in the past. I'm not expecting you to say you love me in return. I *do* believe that you care deeply for me, might even love me. But, to admit that your feelings match mine would form a bond, a commitment, take a step toward a future that you're not prepared to make yet.

"Jillian, do something for me tonight, all right? *Don't say anything.* Just think about what I've told you, knowing it's the truth, that it's honest and real. Think about the fact that from the very beginning, we did *not* have sex, we made love. *Made love,* Jillian. Far more beautiful and intimate, special and rare, than anything I, and hopefully you, have ever experienced before. Think about what you felt as you saw the miracles, the babies that were born tonight, knowing that *our* miracle—the child we would create—is within our reality. Just think and feel."

He kissed her on the forehead. "Good night, Lady Jillian."

Forrest left the bed, dressed quickly and walked out of the room, not looking at her again.

Through the mist of tears filling her eyes, Jillian watched him go, then she buried her face in the pillow and wept, the sobs nearly choking her as tears streamed down her face.

Having no idea how much time had passed, she finally rolled onto her back and pressed the heels of her hands to her now throbbing temples. She drew a shuddering breath, then sighed—a very sad-sounding sigh.

All that she'd accomplished with her wailing, she thought dismally, was to produce a roaring headache. She had to think, sort, sift, deal with all that had happened.

I do love you, Jillian.

"Oh-h-h," she moaned, feeling fresh tears threatening to spill over.

Forrest MacAllister loved her, was *in* love with her. He had, in a roundabout way, said he wanted to marry her, make her his wife, his partner in life, and create the miracle that would be their baby.

Forrest MacAllister loved her, and she loved him in kind.

It was glorious.

No, no, no! It was terrible, a disaster, a frightening scenario in which she could not, would not, take part.

She would *not* tell Forrest that she loved him.

She would *not* place her heart in his hands for safe-keeping, thus rendering herself totally vulnerable.

She would *not* give up the career she'd worked so hard for, and that was a part of who she was.

The price tag for loving Forrest MacAllister was far too high, and more than she was prepared to pay.

Jillian flopped back over onto her stomach, and gave the pillow a solid whack.

"Perdition, Forrest," she said aloud, "why didn't you just stay being The Project, like you were supposed to? You gummed up the whole program."

And so had she, because she'd fallen deeply in love with him.

But he would never know the truth, never know that when he was gone, her heart was going to shatter into a million pieces.

Andrea sat propped up in the hospital bed, a smile of delight on her face as she looked at the two huge teddy bears sitting at the foot of the bed. One was pink, the other blue, and they were grinning to beat the band.

"The bears are wonderful, Forrest," she said. "They're as big as two-year-old children, so they'll have to be decorations in the nursery until the twins are older."

"At least they won't eat you out of house and home," Forrest said, settling onto the chair next to the bed.

"Since you're here at three in the afternoon," Andrea said, "I assume you're still on vacation from the ever famous MacAllister Architects, Incorporated."

Forrest nodded.

"Speaking of famous," she went on, "John told me that Jillian was here at the hospital with you last night."

"She was here," he said quietly.

"You still haven't given me any details of your social life with Jillian, you rotten rat."

Forrest shrugged. "You had other things on your mind. Two little other things, as a matter of fact."

Andrea folded her hands in her lap and studied her brother. Forrest met her gaze for a moment, then directed his attention to the smiling teddy bears.

"Okay, big brother, what's wrong?" she said.

"Wrong?" he echoed, raising his eyebrows as he looked at her again. "Nothing is wrong. What could be wrong? I mean, jeez, I'm the uncle of two new fantastic kids. Miracles. That's great. You're great. You and John are great. Everything is great. I've got such a long list of great, that—"

"Cut," she said, slicing one hand through the air. "This is me, Andrea, remember? I know you very well, sweetheart, and something is most definitely wrong." She paused, narrowed her eyes and nodded. "Jillian Jones-Jenkins."

"You're dreaming."

"I'm right on the money. Talk to me."

"Speaking of money, I'm going to split the bundle I won on The Baby Bet with you. That seems only fair, since you delivered the twins in my predicted order. I'm still The Baby Bet champion, madam."

"Would you cut it out? What's going on between you and Jillian that is causing you to look as dreary as yesterday's oatmeal? It's worse than that. You're as grim as today's lunch they served me in this place. Forrest?"

"Hey, Andrea, I didn't come here to dump on you. You just had two babies, for crying out loud. Take off your sister hat and put on your new-mother hat. Just forget about me."

"Not a chance. Talk to me, or I'll sign you up for diaper duty so John and I can go out to dinner when I've escaped from here."

Forrest opened his mouth, closed it again, and shook his head. He sighed, looked at the ceiling for a long moment, then met Andrea's now troubled gaze.

"I'm in love with Jillian, Andrea," he said, his voice low and not quite steady.

"That *should* be wonderful. You've waited a long time to love, to be in love, fall in love. I know how much you want to have a wife and babies. The fact that you're not turning cartwheels means there's a major glitch in your relationship with Jillian.

"Is it her career, Forrest? She has to be very devoted, able to exercise extremely strict self-discipline. But, as you know because you accepted the Angels and Elves assignment, she works much too hard.''

"No, it's not her writing. There's no problem there at all. I highly respect her talent and what she has accomplished. I've enjoyed reading her books, too. It's a demanding career, but she seems to have a healthy balance in her life of work and leisure. She's on vacation right now, because she decided she needed a break. You and Deedee overreacted to Jillian's schedule.''

"Well, shame on us. That area is apparently in apple-pie order. So? What's wrong?''

"I wouldn't talk about Jillian's private life because it's just that—private—but you don't count.''

"Oh, thanks," Andrea said, laughing.

"You know what I mean.''

"Of course, I do," she said, her expression serious again.

"Jillian was badly hurt years ago by a crummy marriage to a real jerk. She's closed herself off, built protective walls around herself. I knew that, damn it. I knew she was wary and skittish, that I mustn't rush her or do anything to cause her to build those walls higher and stronger.''

Forrest leaned forward, resting his elbows on his knees and making a steeple of his fingers.

"Jillian cares for me, Andrea, I'm certain of that. She might— Well, she might even be in love with me, but is too frightened to tell me, or maybe too scared to even admit it to herself. Hell, I don't know. What I *do* know is that I blew it. Big time. Major league.''

"How?''

"I told her that I loved her. I opened my big, stupid mouth and said that I loved her, wanted to create a miracle, a baby, with her. I didn't come right out and ask her to marry me, but I'm sure my intentions were clear."

"You were being honest and open," Andrea said, nodding decisively. "That's important in a relationship. I think your telling her how you felt was excellent."

"I think it was the dumbest thing I've ever done."

"Oh. Well, what did she say?"

"Nothing."

"Nothing? You declared your love to a woman and she said *nothing?*"

"I wouldn't let her," he said, sinking back in the chair. He dragged a restless hand through his hair. "I blathered on like the idiot of the year, and realized an instant later that I'd made a terrible mistake. Jillian isn't ready to hear that stuff yet. She needs more time, and I should have been patient. I told her not to say anything, but to think about it—everything I'd said. Then I hightailed it out of there, coward that I am. I repeat, I blew it. In spades."

"Oh, dear," Andrea said. "A woman left alone to brood can be a dangerous creature. We have very active minds, you know. It's much better to start the communication process immediately when dealing with a major issue."

"I figured I'd stay out of her way for a few days."

"Wrong. You should see her as soon as possible, then sit her down, and gently—*gently*—say it's time to talk things through."

"Bad plan. I'd rather take on diaper duty for the twins."

"Forrest MacAllister, you really *are* a coward."

"You've got that straight. I'm scared to death, Andrea. I love Jillian and want to spend the rest of my life with her. The thought of losing her just rips me up."

"Go to her, Forrest."

He got to his feet. "You're a tough cookie. John sure does have his hands full being married to you."

"The lucky son of a gun," she said, smiling.

"Yes, he is." He leaned over and kissed her on the forehead.

"Will you do it? Will you go talk to Jillian?"

Forrest nodded. "I have to settle down a bit first, but I'll call her and see if I can set it up for tomorrow night. I'll probably have a complete mental collapse before then, though."

"Talk . . . to . . . her."

"Yeah, yeah, okay, I will." Forrest walked to the end of the bed and stopped, staring at the huge teddy bears. "I'm big, strong, healthy, and prepared to slay the dragons for my Lady Jillian, but my physical strength means nothing. Love sure is an equalizer, a powerful force that has the capability of stripping a man bare."

"And of bringing him the greatest joy he's ever known," Andrea said softly.

Forrest nodded slowly, then turned and left the room.

"Deedee?" Andrea said into the telephone receiver. "Are you sitting down?"

Ten

The following evening, Jillian stood in the kitchen looking at the clock on the wall. The hands seemed to be moving at a snail's pace, inching closer to seven o'clock and Forrest's scheduled arrival.

She'd dressed in jeans, a magenta-colored sweater and matching socks, with the hope that the bright, cheerful attire would improve her dark, gloomy mood.

It hadn't helped one iota.

With a cluck of self-disgust, she stomped out of the kitchen, smacking the light switch to Off as she passed. In the living room, she sank onto the sofa in front of the fireplace and stared at the leaping flames.

She was a wreck. Forrest had called late yesterday afternoon, said they needed to talk, and was seven o'clock the next evening convenient?

He'd sounded stiff, stilted, like someone making an

appointment to sell her life insurance. She'd agreed to the plan, and had been a bundle of nerves ever since.

She couldn't pretend that she didn't know what Forrest wanted to discuss. The man had told her that he was in love with her, for Pete's sake. He'd then proceeded to tell her to think, think, think, about the list of items he'd clicked off. Now the jig was up. This was it. Forrest was coming for answers, responses to what he'd said.

"Oh-h-h, perdition," Jillian said, leaning her head against the back of the sofa.

Snatches of Forrest's words had echoed in her mind through the entire day and on into the evening.

I do love you, Jillian. It's the truth. It's honest and real. When we made love it was far more beautiful, intimate, special and rare, than anything I, and hopefully you, have ever experienced before. Think about the babies, the miracles, knowing our child is within our reality. I do love you, Jillian. I do love you, Jillian. Just think and feel. Think, think, think.

"Oh-h-h," she moaned again, pressing her palms to her aching temples.

She was so muddled, so confused, so incredibly unhappy. It was as though an exhausting tug-of-war was taking place in her mind, yanking her back and forth between fantasy and reality.

The make-believe was glorious. She had no ghosts from the past haunting her, holding her in a fist of fear. She was free to follow the missive from her heart, to tell Forrest that she loved him, wanted to be his wife, and the mother of his children.

In that fantasyland, she didn't have a demanding career that required her full devotion, both emotionally and physically. She wrote books as a hobby. Yes, that was good—a hobby, where she dashed off a paragraph or two when the mood struck.

But reality? Oh, dear heaven, it was totally opposite from that sugarcoated fairy tale. And reality was synonymous with the truth, and the truth was what she would have to convey to Forrest in a very few minutes.

But not the whole truth, she thought glumly. She would not tell Forrest MacAllister that she was in love with him. It would serve no purpose, because the bottom-line fact that they had no future together could not be changed.

The doorbell rang, and Jillian sighed as she got slowly to her feet and started across the living room.

She wished she was anywhere other than on her way to opening the front door. Siberia held appeal, or Afghanistan, or—

"Jillian, shut up," she muttered.

She stopped in the entry hall, took a deep, steadying breath, then opened the door, hoping to heaven that her smile didn't appear as phony as it felt.

"Hello, Forrest," she said, stepping back. "Please come in."

"Jillian," he said, nodding slightly. There was no trace of a smile on his face.

She closed the door and turned to look at him, allowing herself to savor a quick scrutiny of his magnificent physique presented to perfection in jeans and a black turtleneck sweater.

Forrest looked directly into her eyes, placed one hand on her cheek and brushed his lips over hers.

"It's good to see you," he said, dropping his hand to his side.

"Yes, well, it's nice to see you, too. Shall we go in by the fire?"

She hurried past him without waiting for his reply, and Forrest followed slowly behind. Jillian sat down on the sofa and folded her hands in her lap, suddenly wishing she'd mastered knitting so she could busy herself with something other than the tension-filled moment.

Gently, Forrest ordered himself. Andrea had emphasized that he was to discuss the issues at hand gently, talk things through gently. That was going to be a good trick, considering the fact that he was so stressed he felt like a tightly coiled spring that was apt to go rocketing into orbit at the slightest provocation.

He considered settling onto the sofa next to Jillian, then rejected the idea as futile, knowing he was too wired to sit still. Instead, he planted one forearm on the mantel.

Damn, he thought. Jillian looked like a scared kid who had been summoned to the principal's office. Her beautiful gray eyes were wide and wary, her hands clutched tightly in her lap, her magenta-socked feet planted soldier-square on the floor.

The tension in the room was a nearly palpable entity, and for the life of him he didn't know how to defuse it before it exploded into a disaster.

"Hell," he said.

Jillian blinked in surprise. "Hell?"

He shoved his hands into the back pockets of his jeans for lack of a better thing to do with them, and his frown deepened.

"This is really ridiculous," he said. "This is supposed to be a momentous moment, a special occasion in both of our lives, and I feel as though I came to announce that your dog died."

"Well, I—"

"Damn it, Jillian," he said, his volume now on high, "I love you. I want to marry you. Have you got that? Is it loud and clear enough for you?"

He rolled his eyes heavenward.

"That cooked it," he said, shaking his head.

Pulling his hands free of his pockets, he dragged them down his face.

"Okay," he said, crossing his arms loosely over his chest. "I'm in my 'gently' mode. Jillian, do you believe that I love you with all my heart?"

"Yes," she said softly.

"Oh. Well, that's good, great." He paused. "Look, it's so important that you come to grips with your past, deal with it, then put it away. It's the only way you can have the fulfilling present and future that you deserve to have."

"I realize that, but—"

"You do? That's fantastic, terrific." He stepped forward and sat down next to her, shifting on the sofa so he could face her. "That's wonderful, Jillian."

"No, you're misinterpreting what I'm—"

"Jillian, please," he interrupted, raising one hand. "Let me have my say before I botch this up." He covered her hands with his. "I love you, Jillian. There's nothing to be afraid of by admitting that you love me. Maybe that sounds conceited as hell, but you've been the other half of all we've shared, every step of the way. We've grown together, learned so much, put solid bricks into place as the foundation of our relationship."

"But—"

"Shh." He gave her a quick kiss on the lips. "We can have it all, together, if you'll look forward instead of backward. Because *I* trust *you*. I've come to believe that a fulfilling two-career marriage *is* possible. I really listened to what you said about compromises.

"Ah, Jillian, we'll have a home—not just a house, but a home filled with love and the sound of our children's laughter. I won't put in such long hours or bring work home, and your career isn't a stumbling block, so—"

"Halt." She slipped her hands free of his and raised them, palms out. "Whoa. Why isn't my career a stumbling block?" She crossed her arms under her breasts.

Forrest frowned, confusion evident in his expression.

"It's very simple," he said, with a shrug. "I respect what you do more than I can even tell you. That's important, you know, that a husband and wife respect each other's work. I don't feel threatened by your success, or by your ability to support yourself on a financial level."

"And?"

"And what?"

"Forrest, my novels don't write themselves. It takes me months to complete a book."

"Oh, that."

Jillian narrowed her eyes. "Meaning?"

"Well, holy smoke, what's the problem? It's been obvious to me from the day I met you that you have a healthy balance in your life of work and leisure time.

"You needed a vacation, so you took one. You're a professional, who's organized, intelligent, the whole nine yards. I can't imagine you having any difficulty revamping your writing schedule to include hearth, home, husband and kids.

"I'd do my share, you know, be right in there pitching. I could hold down the fort if you went on an autographing tour, or whatever. Your writing wouldn't get in the way of anything."

Jillian jumped to her feet, and Forrest jerked in surprise.

"Get in the way?" she shrieked, her hands curled into fists at her sides.

"What are you getting stressed-out about? All I'm trying to do is show you that I've changed my opinion on two-career marriages, and it's possible for us to have a wonderful life together. We'll iron out the nitty-gritty details and go for it. There's nothing standing in our way, Jillian."

Emotions slammed against Jillian's mind in a brutal attack, causing a momentary wave of dizziness to sweep over her.

The fears born of past pain were there, as well as the aching chill of knowing she was in love with Forrest but had no room for him in her life.

And anger. Oh, the fury, the rage. Forrest MacAllister, she fumed, was dismissing her career as incidental, something that could be worked in around the edges, something *that wouldn't get in the way of anything*.

"Jillian?" Forrest said tentatively. "What's going on, here? You look mad as hell, but I sure don't understand why."

"You don't understand *anything*," she said, none too quietly. "You've had your say, Forrest MacAllister, and now I'll have mine, so listen up. Maybe, just maybe, I could have put the past behind me in regard to the pain I suffered in my marriage. But there's no point in dwelling on that 'maybe,' because it's not the major issue here."

"It isn't?"

"It sure as hell isn't, buster."

"Buster? You *are* mad as hell. What did I do? What did I say wrong to set you off?"

"I am a woman," she said, splaying one hand on her breasts, "and I am a writer, a published author. The writer part of my being is intricately entwined with the woman. Without my writing, I wouldn't be complete, whole, the total essence of who I am.

"My work, Mr. MacAllister, my writing, does not get penciled in on the calendar when I'm in the mood. It's my focus, my purpose, my center, my life. Everything else takes second seat."

"But—"

"You just happened to meet me when I was starting a two-week vacation—fourteen days, and not one hour more. Those vacations only happen two or three times a year. The remainder of the time, I work.

"I'm in my office eight, ten, even twelve hours a day. I rarely see anyone, or go anywhere. I'm totally immersed in the story I'm writing, in the characters. I laugh with them, cry with them, become them, in order to make them alive and real to the people who read my books. I have no room for anything or anyone else during those months."

"Holy smoke," Forrest whispered, staring at her with wide eyes. "I thought—"

"I know what you thought," she rushed on. "A vacation would be nice? Oh, what the heck, I'll just take two weeks off. Have a baby? Tend to a house? Hey, no problem. My little hobby of writing books could be juggled into the system someplace. You're so off base, MacAllister, it's a crime."

Forrest lunged to his feet. "Why didn't you tell me all of this before? You led me to believe—"

"No! You drew your own conclusions. I was following my strict vacation rules for stepping away from my world of writing. I was concentrating on what Andrea and Deedee convinced me to take on as The Project, what they called an Angels and Elves assignment. They felt you were focusing all your energies on work, and needed to be shown how to relax, have fun."

Oh, dear heaven, no! she thought frantically. She hadn't meant to say that, to bring up the subject of The Project. It would sound so terribly cold and calculating, so unfeeling.

Forrest stiffened, every muscle in his body tightening to the point of actual pain.

"The project?" he repeated, his voice ominously low. "The rules of your vacation call for you to put space between yourself and your writing, to take on a 'project,' and *I* was it for your little hiatus this time?

"Well, guess what. Andrea and Deedee convinced *me* to take *you* on as *my* Angels and Elves assignment because they were worried about how hard you were working."

"They were matchmaking, being Cupids," Jillian said, her eyes widening.

"Bingo. I'd give them a heavy-duty piece of my mind about their scheme, but I believe they did it out of genuine caring. The thing is, in my case what they hoped would happen actually came to be. I fell in love with you. But you? Ah, damn it, Jillian, you—" He stopped speaking and shook his head.

Jillian pressed trembling fingertips to her lips as she watched Forrest stare up at the ceiling for a long moment, struggling to control his emotions. When he looked at her again, she felt instant tears burn her eyes as she saw the anger in his brown eyes change to stark, raw pain.

"It was all a game to you, wasn't it?" he said, his voice flat. "A project, an Angels and Elves deal, something to do to keep from being bored while you took time off from work."

"Forrest—"

"God, what a fool I've been," he went on, self-disgust ringing in his voice. "How did you keep a straight face, not fall on the floor laughing, when I talked about wanting to marry you, have babies with you, spend the rest of my life with you?"

He dragged one hand through his hair.

"Oh, hey, I've got it." He snapped his fingers. "This was all research for your next book. Right? Well, you'll have some sizzling love scenes to put on paper. No, correct that. *Sex* scenes. That's what it was to you—just casual sex."

"Forrest, no," she said, tears filling her eyes. "Please, it wasn't a game, or research, I swear it wasn't." Two tears spilled onto her pale cheeks.

"Tears, Lady Jillian?" There was, a bitter edge in his voice. "Nice touch. You're an actress, as well as a famous author."

He paused.

"No..." he said slowly. "I think this whole number is more complex than it appears. I think you're playing games with yourself, as well."

"What...what do you mean?" she said, dashing the tears away.

"You're hiding, Jillian. You were hurt once, and you're so damn scared of it happening again that you're using your writing as an excuse not to square off against life and the risks people run if they embrace it. You're so terrified of reality that you live your life through make-believe characters."

"That's not true."

"Isn't it? You can control those characters, decide on everything they'll say, guarantee them a happy ending by having them do exactly what you dictate. You venture out into the real world for a couple of weeks here and there, then hightail it back behind your protective walls, hole up in your office where it's safe.

"You transport yourself back in time to another era as an extra precaution against the 'now' of your existence being able to touch you. You don't allow anyone into that space, that place in history, where you exist. Oh, yes, Jillian, you're hiding."

"No!"

"Think about it. Or don't think about it. Hell, I don't care. I've had enough of this."

He turned and started across the room.

"Forrest, wait."

He hesitated, then stopped, shifting slightly to look back at her.

"No, thanks. You're a helluva writer, Jillian. I really believed that truth, trust and honesty were important to you because they were emphasized in every novel of yours I read. What a joke. *I* was a joke to you, too, and that hurts. That hurts like hell.

"I just hope it doesn't take me too long to put you entirely out of my heart and mind, to forget that I love you. I don't think it will be too tough, because the truth of the matter is, I never really knew you at all. It was all a game of make-believe."

He turned again and strode away. A few moments later, Jillian heard the front door slam. She flinched as the loud noise reverberated through the house.

"Forrest, don't go," she said, nearly choking on a sob. Tears streamed unchecked and unnoticed down her face and along her neck. "You're wrong. I love you, Forrest MacAllister."

She sank back onto the sofa and buried her face in her hands.

The only sounds in the large room were the crackling flames in the fireplace, and the heartbroken weeping of Jillian Jones-Jenkins.

Eleven

A week later, Jillian shut off the computer and leaned back in her chair, staring at the darkened screen. She glanced at her watch, then got to her feet to roam around her spacious office.

Jillian, she told herself, it's time to gather some data.

She had relived the final encounter with Forrest over and over in her mind, seeing the raw pain in his beautiful brown eyes, hearing his harsh accusations that she was living her life through the characters in her books, even transporting herself back in time, because of her fear of reality and "now."

Her emotions had swung continually back and forth like a pendulum, moving from tear-producing sorrow to rip-roaring anger.

But two facts remained constant: she loved Forrest MacAllister with every fiber of her being, and she missed him with an aching intensity.

Those items, however, were not the topics on which she was presently data-gathering. No, the subject at hand was her work.

The morning after the disastrous evening with Forrest, she'd headed for her office, knowing she still had several vacation days left, but having no desire to be idle.

She hadn't expected to be able to accomplish a great deal of writing due to her emotional upheaval, but found to her surprise that the outline for her new book fell nicely into place.

The next day she'd returned to the office with the mind-set that she was still off duty, didn't have to be there, and, hence, anything she produced would be viewed as a bonus against her future deadline.

To her amazement, she once again was pleased with her output and the knowledge that she'd been able to set aside her personal turmoil the moment she'd stepped inside the room designated only for writing.

In the week that followed, she'd met her daily quota of pages in half the normal time allotted each day. *Half the time!*

Why? she wondered, continuing to wander back and forth across the room.

She stopped and wrapped her hands around her elbows in a protective gesture, having realized that the truth of the answer to the question was stark and painfully revealing.

She had subconsciously, for a very long time, made her day-to-day production schedule take up more hours than were necessary.

"Oh, perdition," she whispered.

Forrest's accusations were right on the mark. She had escaped into her office, into the lives of her characters and the place in history where they existed, rather than face her own reality. She'd been hiding like a frightened child.

"Oh, Jillian, what have you done?"

She'd lost the man who loved her, the man she loved. Her fears had caused her to forfeit a wondrous future with Forrest MacAllister. There would be no marriage, no home overflowing with joy and sunshine, no miracle of a baby created with Forrest.

Tears misted her eyes and she left the office to go to the sofa in front of the warming fire in the living room.

It was all so clear to her now. She'd lived the majority of her childhood in a fantasyland born of her imagination and providing an escape from her loneliness.

When she'd ventured out of her protective cocoon to marry Roger, she'd been betrayed, terribly hurt. So, she'd returned to a world comprised mostly of make-believe, where it was safe, risk free, under her command and control.

She was long overdue to grow up, to behave like the mature woman she professed herself to be. She would muster her courage, defeat the haunting ghosts of the past, and fling them into oblivion forever.

Jillian sniffled, then swept an errant tear from her cheek.

She'd be eligible for high scores in newfound mental health. She'd be the woman she was meant to be; whole, embracing life, functioning as a complete person.

But she would not be with the man she loved!

"Oh, perdition," she said, hiccuping along with a sob. "I love him, I want to spend the rest of my life with the man. I want to have his baby—two babies, four, a whole bunch of babies. I want it all, *and it's too late.* I've lost him. He's gone. And it's all my fault."

If she didn't stop talking aloud to herself, her next stop would be a place with bars on the windows where weird people were kept.

Jillian jumped to her feet and narrowed her eyes.

Wait just a darn minute, here. She'd spent more years than she cared to admit being defeated by her worst enemy—herself. Well, this time she wasn't giving up the battle without a fight. If there was any way possible to share with Forrest the future he'd once wished to have with her, she'd find it, by gum.

Oh, yes, she was ready. Well, she would be, once she figured out a genius-level plan.

Jillian Jones-Jenkins was on the march!

Settling back onto the sofa, she squeezed her eyes tightly closed and began to concentrate on The Plan.

She had a vivid imagination, for heaven's sake. It was time to apply that creativeness to real life. The heroine was intent on winning back the hero. Victory would be hers!

In the late afternoon, one week later, Michael appeared next to Forrest's desk at MacAllister Architects, Incorporated.

"Forrest?"

"What?" he said, not looking up.

"See my face?"

Forrest shifted his gaze to Michael. "It's as ugly as it usually is. What else do you want to know?"

"Whether or not you still recognize this kind of thing," Michael said, pointing to his lips. "It's called a smile. Remember smiles?"

Forrest redirected his attention to the file in front of him. "No." He glanced at his watch. "My day is over. I'm outta here."

"No," Michael said quickly. "You can't leave yet."

"Why not?"

"The phone might ring."

"So answer it, or have our secretary answer it. She's really into answering the phone." Forrest got to his feet. "I hope you didn't pass on your nutso gene to Bobby. Poor little kid. That would be a bum rap. You're strange, Michael, very strange."

The telephone on Forrest's desk rang.

"Ah-ha." Michael pointed to the shrilling phone. "It rang. One should not doubt those who are older and wiser than you, Forrest."

"Bull."

"Answer the damn phone!"

Forrest glared at his brother, then snatched up the receiver. "MacAllister Architects, Incorporated."

"Forrest? It's Andrea."

"Hi, Andrea. How are the munchkins?"

"Phase one of The Plan," Michael said under his breath, as he walked away, "is a done deal."

"The babies are super," Andrea said to Forrest. "I wish they'd get together more on their sleeping routine, though. It seems that when Matt goes to sleep, Noel wakes up."

"I'll speak to them about it," Forrest said. "They'll heed the words of their Uncle Forrest."

"How nice. Listen, you wouldn't happen to be leaving the office now, would you? I mean, I just couldn't possibly know the schedule around there these days. Did I, by some slim chance, get lucky?"

"Yeah, I'm just about to leave."

"Well, fancy that. If you don't have plans for tonight, could you do me a teeny-tiny favor?"

"Andrea, I haven't been able to say no to you from the day you were born, and you know it. What do you need?"

"You're such a sweetheart. John has a business dinner to attend, and Deedee suggested that she and I go out for a quick hamburger. You have no idea how wonderful it sounds, especially if that gourmet meal can't be interrupted by Matt or Noel. Would you come over and stay with the twins?"

"Me? Andrea, I don't know the first thing about taking care of babies."

"There won't be anything for you to do. They'll be fed, diapered, and sound asleep. Guaranteed."

"Yeah, sure," he said dryly.

"Hey, these little guys were the means by which you won The Baby Bet, remember? Would they do something rotten to their favorite uncle?"

Forrest sighed. "Oh, man, I've got to be nuts, but I'll do it. You're lucky I'm even speaking to you, or to Deedee, for that matter, considering the fact your stint as Cupids was a disaster. Your double dose of Angels and Elves assignments failed miserably."

"We're so sorry, Forrest. Deedee and I feel just terrible about what happened between you and Jillian, or what didn't happen, or whatever."

"I don't want to talk about it. I'll be at your place within the hour."

"Wonderful. I'll leave the front door unlocked, so just come on in. I'm going to be putting the finishing touches on my makeup. I'm going to be gorgeous."

"To go eat a hamburger?"

"Mothers of twins do not take the gift of time off lightly. A hamburger calls for 'gorgeous.'"

"If you say so."

"I say so. See you soon. Bye, Forrest."

Andrea replaced the receiver and beamed at Deedee. "Phase two of The Plan," Andrea said, "is a mission accomplished."

"Fantastic," Deedee said.

A circle of warmth tiptoed about Deedee's heart and showed itself as a soft smile as she recalled the long talk she'd shared with Jillian as they sat on the floor in front of the roaring fire at Jillian's house.

Jillian had poured out the sad tale of her marriage and her desire to put those ghosts to rest for all time. She'd talked about her career, and with love shining in her eyes, had spoken of Forrest MacAllister.

Her friendship with Jillian, Deedee knew, had deepened that night, bonded them as sisters.

"The Plan will work, Andrea. It just has to."

The drive to Andrea's was slowgoing due to heavy traffic. Forrest's frustration grew as he was forced to stop at yet another red light, and he drummed his fingers impatiently on the steering wheel.

The light changed and he pressed on the gas pedal.

He'd caught Michael's not-very-subtle reference to his lousy frame of mind. His brother was letting him know by asking him if he remembered what smiles were, that Mr. Forrest MacAllister had not exactly been sunshine itself over the past two weeks.

So, okay, he'd work on his attitude.

It wasn't his family's fault he was a jerk, had lousy taste in women and had misread Jillian Jones-Jenkins from day one.

It wasn't their fault he wasn't sleeping well, had no appetite and was one very miserable man.

It wasn't their fault that he still loved Jillian with every breath in his rapidly depleting body.

No, that wasn't exactly true. He loved the Jillian he'd *believed* her to be, not the one who had eventually shown her true colors. But the image of Jillian, the fantasy, was in his mind's eye every waking hour of the day and night.

Time, he hoped, would ease his pain, his sense of being betrayed, played for a fool, his chilling loneliness. In the interim, he really had to make more of an effort to smile.

He'd start by smiling at the they'd-better-be-sleeping twins. Those babies were really cute. Matt was easygoing, a laid-back little guy, and Noel was on a short fuse. She wanted a dry diaper right now, and something to eat right now, no excuses, thank you very much. Noel definitely took after Andrea.

What would a baby created by Jillian and him have looked like?

"Shut up, MacAllister," he said. "Quit pouring salt in your own wounds."

At last arriving at Andrea and John's, Forrest parked in front and glanced around as he got out of the car. There were no other vehicles in the circular driveway, and he absently deduced that Andrea's car was still in the double garage.

When he came to the front door, he automatically reached out to ring the bell, then halted, remembering Andrea's instructions to enter the house.

"She's getting gorgeous for a hamburger," he muttered. "Women are weird biscuits."

In the entry hall, he stopped, sniffed the air, then frowned.

He'd swear he was savoring the enticing aroma of baking chicken, but that didn't make sense. Why would someone who was about to engage in the thrilling experience of going out for a fast-food hamburger have a chicken cooking in her oven?

No, he wasn't really smelling chicken. He was simply a hungry man ready for his dinner who *wished* there was a chicken turning crispy brown and juicy in the oven.

As Forrest went on into the living room, he pulled off his tie and stuffed it into his jacket pocket. Next he removed the jacket and draped it over the back of a chair.

"Yo, Andrea," he called. "Your nanny is here to watch over sleeping babies. Catch the word *sleeping*, little sister. Are you gorgeous enough for a hamburger yet?" He paused. "Hey, where are you, brat?"

"Hello, Forrest," a soft voice said.

He spun around and his eyes widened in surprise. Opening his mouth to speak, he instantly realized he'd stopped breathing and had to take a gulp of air.

"Jillian?" he finally managed to say, more in the form of a croak.

"Yes, Forrest, it's me . . . Jillian."

He swallowed heavily and the sound of his racing heart echoed in his ears as he scrutinized Jillian from head to toe, drinking in the sight of her like a thirsty man.

She was wearing jeans, a purple sweatshirt with a pink elephant on the front, and purple socks. She was the most sensational woman he'd ever seen, an absolute vision of beauty. And, oh, God, how he loved her.

He took one step toward her, then stopped, a frown replacing his shocked expression.

Hold it, MacAllister, he ordered himself. Think, idiot. He had no idea why she was there, what she was up to, but he wasn't having any, by damn. He'd do well to remember that Jillian Jones-Jenkins had used him, toyed with him, made a complete fool of him. He was older and painfully wiser, in regard to Miss Jones-Jenkins.

"So what's the deal?" he said, striving for an I-really-don't-give-a-damn tone of voice. "Are you joining Andrea and Deedee for a hamburger and fries?"

"No. Andrea isn't home, Forrest. She was at Deedee's store when she telephoned and asked you to baby-sit the twins. I'm the only one here with the babies. For all practical purposes, you and I are alone."

Warning bells went off in Forrest's head, and he narrowed his eyes.

Ho-ho, he thought, the light was dawning. There was a conspiracy afoot. First there had been Michael's crazy demand that Forrest not leave the office as scheduled because the phone might ring. It *had* rung, and there was Andrea with her plea to stay with the twins. Now here was Jillian—alone, obviously having intended to see him while no one else was around.

What were they all up to?

What did Jillian want?

He intended to find out.

But this time he was one step ahead of Jillian's games. He now realized that he'd been duped into coming to Andrea's house. Jillian had rallied the troops for heaven only knew what reason, but he would stay on red alert, follow the dictates of his logical mind, *not* his love-torn heart.

"Okay." He nodded slowly. "It's your ball, Miss Jones-Jenkins."

Oh, thank goodness, Jillian thought, with a rush of relief. Forrest wasn't going to turn around and walk out of the house in a fit of temper. He wasn't smiling—oh, how she yearned to see that gorgeous smile—but he was cooperating. The Plan had to work; it just had to. She loved him so much, so *very* much.

"Could we sit down?" she said.

Forrest swept one arm through the air. "Whatever you say."

He went to a chair, while Jillian sank onto the sofa facing him, grateful that her trembling legs had carried her that far.

"Forrest," she said, wishing her voice was steadier, "I've been coming here to Andrea and John's in the middle of the afternoon for the past week."

He folded his arms across his chest. "Why?"

Jillian gazed at him for a long moment. Forrest's masculinity was again weaving over her and through her, causing the heat of desire to stir within her.

Her breath caught as she saw the well-remembered strength of his beautifully muscled arms. She vividly recalled how she'd felt when she'd been held tightly in his embrace.

And his lips... Oh, dear heaven, it was suddenly so warm in the room. Hot. His hands. How exquisite was the feel of his hands on her breasts, on her entire body.

She'd missed him so much, she wanted to fling herself across the short space separating them and nestle close to his rugged body.

Stop it, Jillian, she admonished herself. She was in the midst of The Plan, and needed all her wits about her.

"Jillian," Forrest said, snapping her back to attention, "I asked you why you've been coming here every day." His frown deepened. "Wait a minute. Your vacation is long since over. How is it that you have time to be here and do whatever it is you've been doing? There's no room in your life for anything but your writing when you're working on a book, remember? You do remember saying that, don't you?''

She nodded. ''Yes, that's exactly what I said and it was true—then.''

This was it, she thought. This was the final stage of The Plan. What happened now would determine her entire future happiness.

She took a steadying breath, squared her shoulders, then lifted her chin.

''Forrest, I know you feel that I betrayed you, used you, viewed you as nothing more than The Project—an Angels and Elves assignment, as you and Andrea call it—to occupy my time during my vacation.''

Forrest's jaw tightened, but he didn't speak as he looked directly at Jillian.

''You *were* my Angels and Elves assignment, just as I was yours. Andrea and Deedee were trying to bring us together out of a sense of love.''

''I realize that,'' he said, a slight edge in his voice. ''I'm not angry at *them*. The fact remains that you're intelligent and—I thought—also sensitive and caring enough to realize that something special and extremely important was happening between us. I *believe* that you knew it, but didn't give a damn. You kept up your phony charade because you still had time to fill before your vacation was over.''

''No! That's not true. Oh, Forrest, I know how it seems to you. I can still hear those horrible things I said to you that last time we were together.''

Forrest dragged one hand through his hair, then leaned forward, resting his elbows on his knees and making a steeple of his fingers.

''I remember everything that was said, too,'' he murmured. ''I wish to hell I could forget.''

Tears stung Jillian's eyes as she heard the pain in Forrest's voice, saw it etched on his face.

"Oh, Forrest, I didn't mean to hurt you," she said, willing herself not to cry. "I was terrified, so frightened. My past held me like a cold, iron fist, and I didn't know how to break free. I was behaving like a child, running from ghosts that existed only in my mind. Forrest, are you really *hearing* me as you're listening? I'm speaking in the past tense. I've conquered those ghosts, Forrest. I truly have."

"I'm glad...for you," he said, straightening again in the chair. "There was a time when I thought those ghosts were the only thing standing in our way." He shook his head. "What a joke. The dragon I could never slay is your career. It's all you want or need."

"You accused me," she went on, her voice trembling, "of escaping from reality into a fantasy world because I was too much of a coward to run the risks of embracing life, even to the point of transporting myself back in time as an extra layer of protection. You said I was living through my characters because it was safer and I was in control."

"I shouldn't have said all that," he said, sounding suddenly weary. "I was hurt, angry, and I lashed out at you."

"Forrest," she said, tears echoing in her voice, "everything you said was true."

"What?"

"I've learned a great deal about myself since that painful scene we had. What I've discovered is not flattering, nor am I proud of myself. I *was* hiding from life, Forrest. I escaped into my writing where it was safe and I couldn't be hurt again. It all became very clear to me while we've been apart."

"And?" he prompted, feeling the increased tempo of his heartbeat. Easy, MacAllister. Jillian wasn't finished talking yet; he hadn't heard everything she had to say. He mustn't hope too much, set himself up for another painful fall. But, oh, damn, how he loved her. "Go on, Jillian."

"There's something I want to be certain you know and believe. Forrest, I knew that I loved you before we parted. That's one of the reasons I was so frightened. Despite my resolve to never love again, I had fallen deeply, irrevocably in love with you. Oh, God, Forrest, I was so scared."

"Jillian?" He got slowly to his feet.

"No, wait," she said, raising one hand. "Please let me finish. A successful author has to be disciplined, write every day, but I now know that I had stretched out my work to fill the hours so I could remain in my protective cocoon. I *do* have space in my life for more than my work and I *want* more. I want *you*. I love you, Forrest MacAllister. I want to be your wife and the mother of our babies, our miracles."

She swept one arm in the air.

"This plan to get you here, which Deedee, Andrea, and Michael helped me put together, is to prove to you that I'm speaking the truth, from my heart, my soul. You have just cause to distrust me, but I hope and pray that I'll be able to convince you that I love you more than I can even say.

"I've been coming here at the end of my workday to have Andrea teach me how to tend to babies. I want to be the best mother I possibly can, and Andrea's been so patient. I can't begin to tell you how wonderful it is to hold Noel and Matt, give them baths, rock them to sleep.

"I've finally put to rest the pain of losing my baby so many years ago. I'm looking to the future with the fervent prayer that someday I'll nestle *our* baby—yours and mine, our miracle—to my breast."

Two tears slid down her cheeks.

"I tried to learn to cook, too, but Andrea finally admitted defeat. I was going to have a delicious dinner waiting for you here, but I forgot to turn the oven on again, and the chicken has only just begun to bake." She threw up her hands. "I'm a complete disaster in the kitchen."

"Jillian . . ."

"I love you, Forrest MacAllister," she said, nearly choking on a sob. "Please forgive me for hurting you, for causing you pain produced by my own cowardice. I love you, Forrest. I do."

"God, you've worked so hard, put yourself through the painful process of dealing with your ghosts. You've torn down your protective walls, rendered yourself vulnerable out of love for me, trust in me. I will never—" Forrest stopped speaking for a moment as his emotions overcame him "—never forget this night and the precious treasures, the gifts you've given me."

No longer fighting against the tears that glistened in his eyes, Forrest smiled.

"Lady Jillian," he said, his voice husky, "if you will grant me the honor of your hand in marriage, I will be the happiest knave in the country, or kingdom, or whatever. Ah, Jillian, marry me. Please.

"No, wait. Before you answer, I want to tell you something. I've grown and changed, too, Jillian. I truly believe that a two-career marriage can be fantastic, rich and deep and real. Compromise. It calls for compromise. Therefore, I'm going on record as saying that I'm a helluva cook and I'll be the chef of this outfit.

"Ah, Jillian, there's nothing we can't handle if we do it together, loving each other for the remainder of our days. Will you marry me? Please, Jillian? Will you be my wife and the mother of my children?"

"Oh, Forrest, yes!"

She flung herself into his arms, and the kiss they shared was long and searing, igniting their passion into hot, consuming flames.

Suddenly Forrest snapped his head up and frowned.

"What's that noise?" he said. "It sounds almost like squeaking kittens."

Jillian laughed. "That's the twins waking up. They'll need a dry diaper and a bottle. Then they'll have to be burped, diapered again, played with a bit, rocked to sleep, and—"

"Got it," he said, matching her smile. "You're the baby expert. I want you to teach me everything you've learned so far about tending to munchkins. I think, though, for the well-being of our family, I'm going to ban you from the kitchen."

"Good plan. Oh, Forrest, I love you."

"I love you too, Lady Jillian."

They walked out of the room with their arms encircling each other, knowing that in their hearts, minds and souls, they were taking the first steps toward a glorious future—together.

"Deedee?" Andrea said into the receiver of the telephone. "I found the most beautiful gown today for Jillian and Forrest's wedding. Oh, and guess what? I'm having the cutest outfits made for the twins to wear to the big event. Noel will be an angel, and Matt an elf.

"The guests will probably think I'm crazy dressing the babies that way for a wedding, but everyone that matters will know how appropriate it is. An angel and an elf—perfect.

"You know, I was thinking about the future. Jillian and Forrest definitely want a family. There's no way Forrest could win The Baby Bet *again* when the time comes— Is there?"

* * * * *

THE BABY BET—*these sexy MacAllister men are so unpredictable . . . we couldn't hold 'em to just one line. Experience the warmth and excitement of the MacAllister clan in both Silhouette Desire and Special Edition. In February 1996, Silhouette Special Edition presents*
FRIENDS, LOVERS . . . AND BABIES!
—Ryan MacAllister's discovery of true love . . . and fatherhood.

COMING NEXT MONTH

#967 A COWBOY CHRISTMAS—Ann Major

Born under the same Christmas star, December's *Man of the Month*, Leander Knight, and sexy Heddy Kinney shared the same destiny. Now the handsome cowboy had to stop her holiday wedding—to *another* man!

#968 MIRACLES AND MISTLETOE—Cait London

Rugged cowboy Jonah Fargo was a Scrooge when it came to Christmas—until Harmony Davis sauntered into his life. Could she get him under the mistletoe and make him believe in miracles?

#969 COWBOYS DON'T STAY—Anne McAllister

Code of the West

Tess Montgomery had fallen for Noah Tanner years ago, but he left her with a broken heart *and* a baby. Now that he was back, could he convince her that sometimes cowboys do stay?

#970 CHRISTMAS WEDDING—Pamela Macaluso

Just Married

Holly Bryant was expected to pose as Jesse Tyler's bride-to-be, not fall for the hardheaded man! But Jesse was a woman's dream come true, even though he swore he'd never settle down....

#971 TEXAS PRIDE—Barbara McCauley

Hearts of Stone

Jessica Stone didn't need help from anyone, especially a lone wolf like Dylan Grant. But Dylan refused to let Jessica's Texas pride— and her to-die-for looks—stand in his way!

#972 GIFT WRAPPED DAD—Sandra Steffen

Six-year-old Tommy Wilson asked Santa for a dad, so he was thrilled when Will Sutherland showed up in time for Christmas. Now if only Will could convince Tommy's mom he'd make the perfect husband for her!

MILLION DOLLAR SWEEPSTAKES (III)

No purchase necessary. To enter, follow the directions published. Method of entry may vary. For eligibility, entries must be received no later than March 31, 1996. No liability is assumed for printing errors, lost, late or misdirected entries. Odds of winning are determined by the number of eligible entries distributed and received. Prizewinners will be determined no later than June 30, 1996.

Sweepstakes open to residents of the U.S. (except Puerto Rico), Canada, Europe and Taiwan who are 18 years of age or older. All applicable laws and regulations apply. Sweepstakes offer void wherever prohibited by law. Values of all prizes are in U.S. currency. This sweepstakes is presented by Torstar Corp., its subsidiaries and affiliates, in conjunction with book, merchandise and/or product offerings. For a copy of the Official Rules send a self-addressed, stamped envelope (WA residents need not affix return postage) to: MILLION DOLLAR SWEEPSTAKES (III) Rules, P.O. Box 4573, Blair, NE 68009, USA.

EXTRA BONUS PRIZE DRAWING

No purchase necessary. The Extra Bonus Prize will be awarded in a random drawing to be conducted no later than 5/30/96 from among all entries received. To qualify, entries must be received by 3/31/96 and comply with published directions. Drawing open to residents of the U.S. (except Puerto Rico), Canada, Europe and Taiwan who are 18 years of age or older. All applicable laws and regulations apply; offer void wherever prohibited by law. Odds of winning are dependent upon number of eligible entries received. Prize is valued in U.S. currency. The offer is presented by Torstar Corp., its subsidiaries and affiliates in conjunction with book, merchandise and/or product offering. For a copy of the Official Rules governing this sweepstakes, send a self-addressed, stamped envelope (WA residents need not affix return postage) to: Extra Bonus Prize Drawing Rules, P.O. Box 4590, Blair, NE 68009, USA.

SWP-S1195

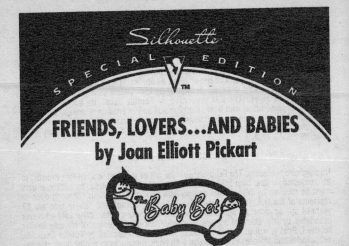

FRIENDS, LOVERS...AND BABIES
by Joan Elliott Pickart

Joan Elliott Pickart brings her own special brand of humor to these heartwarming tales of the MacAllister men. For these three carefree bachelors, predicting the particulars of the MacAllister babies is much easier than predicting when wedding bells will sound!

In February 1996, the most romantic month of the year. Ryan MacAllister discovers true love—and fatherhood—in *Friends, Lovers...and Babies*, book two of THE BABY BET.

And in April 1996, Silhouette Special Edition brings you the final story of love and surprise from the MacAllister clan.

BABBET2

You're About to Become a *Privileged Woman*

Reap the rewards of fabulous free gifts and benefits with proofs-of-purchase from Silhouette and Harlequin books

Pages & Privileges™

It's our way of thanking you for buying our books at your favorite retail stores.

PROOF OF PURCHASE
Offer expires October 31, 1996

SD-PP75

Harlequin and Silhouette—
the most privileged readers in the world!

For more information about Harlequin and Silhouette's PAGES & PRIVILEGES program call the Pages & Privileges Benefits Desk: 1-503-794-2499

™ *Silhouette*®

SD-PP75